Just De

Roderic Jeffries

Table of Contents

Miriam Spiller was middle-aged, plain, and resident on Mallorca, where to the English colony's surprise she had just become engaged. Her fiancé was an unsuccessful novelist – so unsuccessful that he risked deportation if he could not put down a lump sum forthwith to satisfy the Spanish authorities. Miriam talked bravely of borrowing the money for him, but instead she went back to her solitary flat and that night drank too much gin, staggered on to the wrought-iron balcony, and crashed through its rusted railing. A clear case of accidental death.

Except that Brenda Stewart, courier with a tour operator and Miriam's nearest approach to a friend, thought otherwise and passed on her suspicions to the police. And the police were represented by Inspector Enrique Alvarez, whose patient investigation into the manners, morals and past histories of those of Mallorca's English residents who knew Miriam led him into a veritable labyrinth of subterfuge.

Alvarez expected to find crime at its heart, but he never expected to uncover a crime which would affect his own life and happiness.

Chapter One

Blane Cosgrove often thought of Marta as the daughter of the old woman who lived in a shoe: she was short and dumpy, had the heavy, broad face of fecundity, and possessed an easy-going nature except when she had had a row with her husband or one of her children, of whom she appeared – to judge by the stream of names – to have an endless number ... But perhaps many of them were merely nephews or nieces.

'Good morning, señor,' she said, as she crossed the pool patio to where he stood. 'I have brought you an ensaimada. Will you eat it now?' She always began by speaking slowly to help him understand, but if she had a lot to say she ended in a rush of words which left him guessing at their meaning.

'Thanks a lot, but I had breakfast a while back so I'll leave it just for the moment.'

As always, she seemed surprised that he should forgo the chance to eat. She looked up at the clear, sun-blasted sky. 'Water is becoming scarce. In the village it is now cut off every night and perhaps it will be like it was when my grandfather was young and all the wells failed: even his. He had to sell the land to pay his debts. But for that we should now have many cuarteradas of good soil and we would be rich, like the foreigners.' She laughed, as if the loss could occasion only amusement. 'The water is becoming low in the deposito and I will ring for two lorry-loads and tell them to come immediately. They are very busy, but my cousin works for the old man and he will arrange.'

So much was arranged through cousins that he sometimes wondered what happened to foreigners unlucky enough to have no maids with cousins. Perhaps they were those who returned to their countries of origin, cursing the Mallorquins and Mallorca.

She retreated into the house and he moved to his right and leaned over and pulled up the pool thermometer. It was already recording a temperature of 83°F and by the middle of the afternoon this would have risen to 85°F: even so, the water would feel cool to the body.

He straightened up and looked around himself with the pride of ownership. Beyond the pool patio the garden was filled with colour: hibiscus with single and double blooms in red, pink, and apricot, datura shrubs a cascade of white trumpets, orange and lemon trees with the dark green leaves of the previous year and the light green ones of this year, their hard, knobbly fruits just beginning to swell, the bougainvillaea which covered the walls of the pool house with a cascade of dark red and rusty brown bracts, the hedge of red and white oleanders ... And beyond the hedge the almond and fig trees, and the vines with grapes darkening and developing a bloom ... A far, far cry from the garden in the overgrown village of Besham Without, with its laburnums, hydrangeas, roses, and dusty privet hedges. In the semi-detached to which that garden belonged, did Rachael still spend her life fussing over the fluff on the carpets, twitching at the curtains to make them hang more neatly, polishing the dining-room table, and nagging the two children into washing, brushing their teeth, and blowing their noses instead of sniffing?

His thoughts returned to the present. It was a pity that he had accepted an invitation to drinks for lunch, because otherwise he and Gina could have spent the day together. Nothing made a man feel so tall as to be afloat in his own boat with an ice-cold drink in one hand and a red-hot blonde in the other ...

A car crunched its way into the bottle-shaped drive on the other side of the house, and he wondered who the caller could be, since few English stirred this early in the morning. A couple of minutes later Marta returned to the pool.

'It is the señora,' she said abruptly, not bothering to disguise her sense of disapproval.

'Which señora?' he asked patiently.

'The large one with much wealth on her body and no manners,' she answered loudly.

He immediately identified Agnes. 'OK, I'll come on in.' He said to himself; remember, softly, softly, catchee monkey.

He crossed to the covered patio and opened the french windows to go inside. The dining-room and sitting-room formed an L, with the smaller dining-room separated by an archway. Both rooms were furnished with the simple charm which came from natural taste and plenty of money: on the walls hung several paintings by local artists, most of which made up for their artistic shortcomings by a happy extravagance of colour.

8

Agnes Newbolt sat sprawled out in one of the rust-coloured armchairs, her thick legs wide apart, careless of how far up them her beautifully cut frock had ridden. There was a look of impatient discontent on her very fleshy face, particularly about her thick, overhung lips. Today she was wearing her blonde wig with a multitude of tight curls, and if there had not been so much hard, unyielding character in her face it would have made her look embarrassingly like an aged sybarite desperately and pathetically striving for a youth carelessly thrown away.

'What a wonderful surprise!' he said cheerfully. 'The maid told me I had a visitor and I come in to discover she's my favourite girl-friend.' He possessed an easy, saloon-bar charm which many older women found attractive. 'What can I offer you to drink – how about a coffee?'

'I don't want anything,' she replied with the abruptness of someone who never considered anyone but herself.

'It's not Lent, so change your mind? Have an ensaimada and coffee: Marta keeps bringing me an ensaimada in the morning, even though she knows full well I always have breakfast before she gets here and I don't like anything afterwards.'

She ran her peculiarly pink tongue along the underside of her top lip. 'Has it got cream on it?'

'I rather doubt it.'

Her disappointment was obvious.

'But as a substitute I can offer butter and apricot jam.'

'All right,' she said finally.

'I'll go and fix things up: shan't be a moment.'

Marta was not in the kitchen, and almost immediately after he entered the water pump started with its characteristic shrill whine and he could judge that she had begun to water the vegetables which she insisted on growing in one corner of the garden – to grow only flowers was, in her eyes, to be wholly improvident. He put water on to boil – even though both well and bought water were probably quite safe, he always boiled any which was to be drunk – and then put the ensaimada on a plate and the plate on a tray together with butter and jam. He smiled as he made the coffee. Like all really rich people, he thought, Agnes suffered from one fatal weakness – she was so certain that everyone was after her money.

He carried the tray through to her. She pulled off a large piece of the ensaimada – a feathery light confection made from flour, eggs, yeast, lard, and sugar – and spread it very liberally with butter and then coated the

9

butter with jam. When she lifted it up to her mouth some of the jam spilled down over her chin. Never a woman to waste food, she used her left forefinger, on which was the smallest of the three diamond rings she was wearing, to wipe the jam off her chin: she licked the jam from her finger. She swallowed, drank some coffee, then said belligerently, as she buttered another piece of ensaimada: 'You know what I'm here to talk about.'

'Frankly, I haven't the faintest idea.'

She snorted. 'You don't pull the wool over my eyes.'

'It would take a much smarter man than me to do that.'

She stuffed the large piece of ensaimada into her mouth and then somehow found room around it to speak. 'I know what you're after – you're trying to keep everything for yourself.'

He took a cigarette from his thin gold case and lit it.

'But you haven't enough money to complete the deal on your own, have you?'

'Deal?' he said, one eyebrow lifted in ironic questioning.

She waved the knife at him. 'D'you think I don't know what's going on? You've found some land on the sea you reckon would be worth a fortune with development permission, but the local authorities won't grant it. Yet you think there's a chance it may eventually be given.' She paused to refill her mouth. 'What makes you so certain it will be granted?' Her words were now muffled.

He took the cigarette from his mouth and stared at it as he held it in his right hand. The smoke curled upwards, hardly affected by air movement. He looked quickly at her, then back at the smoke.

She leaned forward, her generous bosom sweeping over the remaining portion of ensaimada so that the dress became dusted with icing sugar. 'What have you heard?'

He shrugged his shoulders as he spoke with humorous resignation. 'I've always been told that on this island a dark secret is something which isn't generally known for at least twelve hours ... All right, there is some land.'

'What have you heard?' she demanded for the second time, a suggestion of irritation in her voice.

'Enough,' he answered cryptically.

'Is there a lot of land?'

'Enough,' he said once again, this time sardonically.

'There's nowhere left on the island that's worth developing which hasn't been developed already,' she said challengingly.

'There are dozens of coves without a house on them.'

'Because they're totally inaccessible.'

'This one's inaccessible ... Until one's built a road three-quarters of a kilometre long.'

'Why hasn't it already been built?'

'Where's the point? Officially there's not the slightest likelihood of development ever being allowed.'

She stared belligerently at him for a while, then looked down at the tray. She was surprised to discover that there was still some ensaimada left on the plate. She buttered this, added jam, and pushed it into her mouth. 'And unofficially – what are the odds?'

'Impossible to say with any accuracy.'

'You expect me to believe that?' she snapped scornfully. 'If you hadn't made a very good estimate, you wouldn't be interested in the deal.'

He said nothing.

'How much is the land going to cost?'

'Thirty million.'

'Thirty million!' she repeated, startled.

'To buy it ... and to "persuade" one or two people where their true interests lie.'

'How much is there?'

'The section that's for sale amounts to just on two hundred thousand square metres. It's part bottom land and part hillside which is shallow enough to take buildings. The owner knows quite well what it would fetch if it had development permission, so he's asking ten times what it's presently worth. Like all Mallorquins,' he added ironically, 'he's a profiteer by instinct.'

'Are you intending to go on and develop it?'

'That would cost far more than I could begin to raise. No, there's a Danish company I've heard about ... ' He became silent.

The potential profits could be so great that even with all her wealth she found the prospect immensely exciting. 'How much can you raise?'

He looked quizzically at her. 'Isn't that rather a personal question?'

She waved her right hand in a brief gesture of contempt for such susceptibilities.

'Perhaps half,' he finally answered.

'Then what you need is someone who'll put up fifteen million pesetas?'

'Not so.'

'How d'you mean?'

'If I can't raise the money on my own, I'll forget the deal. I'm not looking for any partners.'

She ignored his answer. 'I'll put in half,' she said abruptly, her beady eyes bright with greedy excitement.

'Sorry, Agnes, but I like you too much ever to let you risk losing fifteen million pesetas – which is what it would amount to if planning permission never does get granted.'

'You don't fool me for one second. All you're interested in is grabbing everything for yourself.'

He made no answer.

'Make me a partner,' she demanded peremptorily.

'No way.' His voice was now crisp and assured. 'I always remember the old tag: "Never do business with an old friend or you'll make a new enemy".'

Her resentment was tinged with bewilderment.

Chapter Two

Halfway along the Laraix valley, Ca'n Blat was a large three-hundred-year-old stone-built house which had been lovingly restored and modernized by a retired American architect who had sadly died shortly after the work had been completed. Agnes had bought the house and two acres of land from the widow. Despite her instinctive predilection for ostentation, Agnes had not succeeded in destroying the charm of the house, but she had ruined the garden. When she had moved in, this had been an apparently haphazard jumble of trees, shrubs, flowers, and grass, which seemingly by some fortunate miracle delighted with endless quiet corners of beauty: failing to recognize the subtle planning which had made the garden what it was, she had decided to redesign it. Three men had laboured for six months and at the end of this time everything had been regimented so that there were no longer any surprises, only too much of everything: including a large pool and a complex of changing rooms, barbecue pit, bar, kitchen, and covered dining area.

She employed two women in the house and one man in the garden and treated them as servants which, since they were Mallorquins, made them laugh at her for her pretensions. She also employed, on a part-time basis, an English secretary.

Miriam Spiller had lived in lower-middle-class England until she was fifty, and in consequence had learned to respect wealth almost as much as royalty and such aristocracy as was untainted by bastardy for at least three generations. She treated Agnes with great respect, at times not untinged with deference and even uneasy servility. She was a tall, thin woman, so austerely plain that even the proverbial Frenchman would have found difficulty in choosing one physical feature to praise. There had been times when she had looked in a mirror and wondered if God really were a benevolent old gentleman with a long white beard and not a crusty misogynist with a spiteful sense of humour.

Her office in Ca'n Blat was on the first floor and through the small window she could see the hills and mountains which ran along the eastern side of the valley. She loved the mountains. They were always changing colour, now slate grey, now dark grey with a mauve tinge; and always changing mood, now welcoming, now hostile. She had never climbed them, but she believed – with a childish disregard of all logic – that from their crests one could look out over a perfect world in which everyone was happy. She had tried to explain this to Frank once, but he had laughed at her for being so stupid. That was the only time when she had momentarily wondered if perhaps he were not quite as brilliant a writer as he said ...

A shout jerked her back to the present. 'Miriam.' She hastily gathered up her notebook. 'Just coming, Mrs Newbolt.' She found the pencil she wanted and hurried downstairs to the library. This was a long, narrow room, beautifully cool in the summer. Two of the walls were lined with built-in bookshelves filled with books, and when she'd first entered it she'd been astonished by the range of Agnes's interests. Later, when she had come to understand Agnes better, she had realized that all the books had been bought from the previous owner's wife solely because they created a good impression.

'You've been a devil of a long time,' complained Agnes. Her desk was beautifully proportioned and had she ever realized the extent of the contrast between it and herself she would have been humiliated. 'I've collected the mail from the village and there's a reply from Smith and Chandler. They haven't answered one of my queries. You must have mistyped my letter.'

'I can't have done that, Mrs Newbolt. And you read the letter through before signing it ... '

'I did not. I had to go out and very stupidly left you to sign it on my behalf.'

She suddenly remembered that this was so. 'But I promise you that I typed out exactly what you dictated.'

'You can't have done or they'd have answered my query.'

She submissively apologized.

'Come on, then, let's get down to work. We can't waste the whole morning worrying over your inefficiency.'

She took dictation for half an hour and then returned to the office. She sat down at the electric typewriter, inserted headed paper, carbon, and copy paper, adjusted the setting, but then paused and stared out of the window at the crests of the mountains as she imagined the perfect land beyond, where no one was ever bullied ...

A tiny wisp of white, not large enough to be called a cloud, appeared above one of the crests. Like a solitary snowflake, she thought, guiltily certain that Frank would contemptuously consider that a ridiculous simile.

Frank. Incredible now to look back and realize that if three years ago she had not done something she still found difficult to believe she had, she would not now be engaged to him. Three years ago she had always been alone even when in the office with all the rest of the staff: now she was never alone, even when on her own.

Frank. One day people would learn to appreciate his books and then he would rightly become truly famous ... If only she could enjoy them; but her schooling had been limited and her tastes were not sophisticated. She liked romances, and not even his caustic criticism of such books was enough to stop her reading them.

She sighed. She looked down at her notebook and began to type.

Chapter Three

'Not bad,' said Carol Davidson. She rolled over on to her side and stared at Frank Finnister as he lay on his back. 'Not at all bad for an old man.'

He nodded complacently.

She leaned over and kissed him. 'D'you know something? I love you. L U V, as I used to spell it.' She began to fiddle with the hairs on his chest, twirling them into spirals. 'Perhaps it's because you're so hairy!'

'When I was living in Bradford ... 'He stopped.

'Go on.'

'A girl I knew called me monkey.' It was clear that the memory still hurt.

'Silly bitch! Anyway, I simply love one monkey.' She leaned over and took one of the spirals between her teeth and pulled and when he yelped she laughed. She loved the matted hair on his chest, the way his chin shadowed so soon after shaving, the hairs which peeked slyly out of his ears, and the way his head was balding in a V, as if the competition from the rest of his body was too great. She loved his pale blue eyes, which so often looked resentfully bewildered, his stubby nose, his sensuous mouth with thick, curving lips, his square chin which was so poor a guide to character, and his prominent Adam's apple which shot up and down whenever he was excited or scared. 'D'you love me, Frank?' she asked.

'Yes.'

'You don't sound very certain?'

'Of course I am.'

She kissed him again. 'I know you are and I'm just teasing you because you don't like putting it into words. It's funny, that.' She snuggled up against him, despite the heat. 'I mean, you being kind of bashful with words when it's your job. I'd have thought you'd've taken a chapter telling me how much you loved me!'

'What's the time?'

'Time you told me you love me in three thousand words.'

'I've got to know the time.'

'Why?'

'I said I'd be at Miriam's at five.'

16

'Goddamn it, why drag her into the conversation?'

'I'm sorry.'

'I've told you again and again, stop apologizing.' She ran her hand down his chest, pausing to tweak the two spirals of hair which remained intact.

He yelped.

'You need looking after like a kid.' She ran her lips across his forehead. 'But Miriam won't look after you: all she knows about are "dear sirs" and "yours very faithfullys".'

'I can't help it if I'm marrying her.'

'Who said you could? And in any case, I'm lumbered with Ted, so who am I to talk?' She rested her head on his shoulder. 'D'you know what it'll be like when I get back home? He'll have started on the bottle. And I'll try to stop him drinking too much but by midnight he'll be pig-drunk and I'll lie in bed and listen to him grunting ... Why's life so bloody unfair? Why can't Ted clear off with Miriam and leave you and me together? Or why couldn't we have met each other before we met them? Just look how things are going to be. Me married to a drunk and you married to a woman who'll undress in the bathroom after she's locked the door.'

'I've got to marry her.'

'But not for the usual reason, that's for sure! Forget it, love. For most of us the world's a bloody place and we can't do a damn thing about it. And you and me haven't really all that much to complain about – we'll always have each other.'

'But after I'm married ... '

'You try to stop seeing me, Frank, and I'll teach you just what a jealous woman will do!'

'But it may not be so easy. I mean, where will we go? You won't be able to come to her flat ... '

'I'm not losing you, not if we have to end up on the beach, getting sand in the works ... Don't you understand, Frank, you're all I've got? Every time Ted gets pig-drunk, every time I have to clear up the mess, every time he belts me ... Did you know he hits me?'

'No,' he answered uneasily.

'It's all right, I'm not going to ask you to belt him in return.' She laughed, but this time there was sadness in her laughter. Ted was six-foot-plus tall, almost as broad, and when sober he feared no one. Frank was five feet seven tall when he held his head high, one had to look hard to locate his shoulders, and either sober or drunk he feared anyone and everyone.

'You could complain to the guardia,' he said.

'And get Ted really ratty? Didn't you know that marriage and wife-beating go together, like apple pie and ice-cream?'

'If only ... ' he began, then stopped.

She knew from his tone of voice what he'd been going to say. Dutifully, she said: 'One day, love, people will really get to reading your books.'

'They won't all the time the publishers treat me like a pariah.'

'Couldn't you, like, maybe change your style a little?'

'Did Zola change his when people objected to what he wrote?'

She'd no idea.

'Profits: the false god of modern literature.'

'I reckon it's most people's god today, love, false or otherwise.' She got off the bed. The curtain across the door was drawn and the shutters of the single window fastened, but enough light came through clearly to outline her. Her features were of the kind usually described as brassy, but when she smiled at Frank there was no hardness in them. Her body was lushly ripe.

She dressed and went over to the window, unclipped the shutters and pushed them back. Sharp, burning sunshine streamed into the small room. 'I'll just nip into the bathroom and give myself a new face.' She picked up her handbag and then looked at her watch. 'You've plenty of time, so no panicking.'

When she returned, mouth newly lipsticked and face carefully powdered, only the lingering glow in her eyes recorded the violent passion she had so recently enjoyed. She kissed him and ran her fingers tenderly over his body. 'When do we see each other again, love?'

'Miriam will be working tomorrow as usual.'

'Then I'll be along here at the same time. Look after yourself, won't you, and do eat properly.'

She kissed him again, crossed to the door, pulled back the curtain, looked back once more and smiled, then left. He heard the outside wooden stairs creak as she went down to the road.

He swivelled round on the bed to a sitting position, reached for a pack of cigarettes, and tapped out a cigarette which he lit. He smoked.

He'd been persecuted all his life. School had been a misery because the other boys had bullied him unmercifully. In his first job he'd worked like a black, but the office manager had been one of those degenerates who resented scholarship. The many literary competitions he'd entered had been judged by men of infinitely pedestrian minds. Vera had promised to love, honour, and obey him until death did them part, but she had gone off with a door-to-door salesman with an RAF moustache and an affected accent. His books, distillations of universal knowledge, were either rejected or, occasionally, accepted and then left deliberately unpromoted, to end their days on the job lot trays of Oxfam shops ...

He looked at his watch and hurriedly stubbed out the cigarette. It was ten to five and Miriam had asked him to be at her flat at five. It was just his luck to have found the one woman in Mallorca who really cared what the time was.

He did not bother to lock up when he left: apart from his latest script, there was nothing in the flat worth stealing. He went down the creaking stairs and his landlady, slowly rocking herself into senility, called out a greeting from the front doorway of her flat. The old bitch. She was trying to put his rent up by two thousand pesetas a month on the grounds that the flat overlooked the bay and in the season any tourist would pay tens of thousands of pesetas for such a choice situation.

He walked along the sea front, past the western arm of the harbour and the large car park, and came to a hot dog and ice-cream stand, where he bought a vanilla cornet. He slowly ate it. Across the road was a hotel and behind that was the block of apartments, in one of which Miriam lived. Was Carol right when she claimed that Miriam was only marrying him in order to be able finally to flaunt a wedding ring before the world? Possibly. Miriam had an infinite capacity for being emotionally stupid.

He was 53 and he had stopped paying national health insurance when he left the UK. This meant that when he was 65 he would be given only a derisory pension. He had no capital. Even a writer had to live, and recently he'd begun to think that perhaps success might not come to him until after he was dead. Penury was a terrifying prospect, and, terror-stricken, he'd wondered about Miriam.

To his surprise she'd met his advances with lady-like approval, and before long they'd become engaged. But now he wondered if, far from providing a way out of his troubles, this marriage might not turn out to be just one more example of life's vindictive persecutions of him ...

He finished the cone and crossed the road, which was temporarily free of traffic, went down the side road to the main entrance of the apartment block. The lift, for once in working order, took him up to the fourth floor. Miriam greeted him with a quick peck on the cheek, which was as near to passion as she ever ventured. 'You look a bit tired, dear,' she said. 'Have you been doing too much?'

'As a matter of fact, I have been hard at it all day,' he answered.

'You must learn to take things more slowly or you'll strain yourself.'

They went through to the sitting/dining-room: quite large and airy, she had used some of the plainer Mallorquin furniture to give the room a pleasant character. She sat, carefully smoothing her longish skirt over her legs. 'Frank, you're looking so worried. Are you sure there's nothing wrong – apart from your having been working too hard?'

He slumped down on the second armchair. 'As a matter of fact ... No, I can't burden you with my troubles.'

'Don't be so silly. Your worries are now my worries.'

'Yes, but ... You know I told you that my two years were up and I'd applied for a new residentia?'

'Yes.'

'This time I had to get my bank to write down how much money I've brought into the country during the past year and how much was in my account on that day.'

'Why?'

'The authorities seem to be trying to weed out foreigners who aren't bringing in enough money to be "respectable".' He spoke with heavy scorn. Then his tone became plaintive. 'I had rather a bad year last year.'

'D'you mean you didn't really bring sufficient into the country?'

'Two detectives came to the flat to check up on me. And because I'm not living in a large villa with a pool and a couple of servants they treated me with contempt. They said that if I didn't bring capital into the country within the next three months, I'd be forced to leave.'

'Leave?' she said, shocked.

'I'd have to go back to England.'

'But that's impossible. What about us? I can't go back to England. I can't leave the island,' she said wildly.

He briefly wondered why she had suddenly spoken with such passion, but did not pursue the problem. 'I've been wondering ... I hate asking, but there's no other way ... Miriam, will you lend me the money which I can bring over and make out I've earned it? If I can satisfy their mean little minds now, I'll be all right for the next two years.'

'How much do you need?'

'One of the detectives said I ought to be bringing in at least three hundred thousand pesetas a year. But I'm sure it'll be enough if there's a couple of hundred thousand in the next three months. And when my present book is taken and properly presented so that it sells, I'll pay you back every penny – together with the interest.'

'Frank, dear, if I'd got that much I'd give it to you immediately. But I haven't.'

He stared at her and for one ridiculous moment thought she was joking. The flat was comfortable, if not luxurious. She never hesitated to buy new clothes. She often suggested they went out to dinner (she handed him the money before they went). For his birthday, she had ordered from England three very expensive reference books ... He'd naturally always assumed that she had a small fortune tucked away in the UK in tax-free government bonds. But if she had no worthwhile capital ...

Her voice became plaintive. 'If I had the money, Frank, I'd give it to you, of course I would. But it used up all my capital to buy this flat and now all I have is my pension.'

'Then I'll have to return to England.'

'But I told you, I can't leave here.'

He shrugged his shoulders.

'Don't you care?' she demanded shrilly.

He looked at her and noticed the lines in her face and wondered how much older she really was than she admitted. 'It's not a case of caring or not caring. If I don't pay in those two hundred thousand, I'll be kicked out of Spain.'

'Surely the bank will lend you that much?'

'With the security I can offer? In any case, I told you, I've got to bring the money into the country.'

'I meant your English bank.'

'They wouldn't lend me a quid to save me from starving.'

She said suddenly: 'I'll find that money for you.'

'How can you, if you've no capital?'

'I know a ... a friend who'll give it to me.'

She obviously expected him to thank her profusely, but he still could not overcome his resentment at discovering that she had no capital worth speaking about.

Chapter Four

Brenda Stewart was told of her husband's death at five-thirty on a quiet, lazy summer afternoon. Initially she had refused to believe the middle-aged police sergeant, who had been sympathetic and yet at the same time chillingly matter-of-fact, but then he had mentioned the Churchill gun and the German Shorthaired Pointer which was standing guard over the body ...

Once the sense of shock eased, she experienced a chilling sense of guilt. If only she had realized that his depression had been so very much more acute than she had judged it, she could have protected him from the mental hell which had engulfed him ... But the doctor had said that for his own sake he must pull himself together and that she mustn't become his sole support ...

Because the bank had been pressing hard for some time, the estate had been sold, though not yet handed over, on the day he died. So she had had to leave the Queen Anne house, redolent of graceful happiness, and the large garden which she had redesigned, and the fields in which the sleek Friesians grazed and heavy crops grew, and the woods in which, although he had been a very keen shot, only crows, jays, magpies, and grey squirrels were killed, so that throughout the year they resounded to bird-calls. To close her eyes was to remember the cooing of pigeons, the harsh cries of cock pheasants, the liquid trills of nightingales. Seventeen years of wonderfully happy married life.

People had called Gerry weak. Their judgements had been as wrong as they were superficial. He hadn't been weak, merely unworldly, unable to understand that today there was only one way in which to survive – pull the ladder up, Jack. If he'd been weak he would never have guaranteed the debt of his oldest friend, who had believed himself so clever a financier and had invested very heavily in a property company, because he would have been scared of the liability. It was his strength of character, his strongly held but very old-fashioned ideas of friendship, which had made him ignore the risks to himself in helping his friend. And when he had understood the full consequences of what he had done he had committed suicide because he believed that that was the only way in which he could make amends, and not because he had been too scared to face the consequences.

She had needed all her courage during the first year after his death. There had been the guilt, the hopelessness, the memories of life amid quiet beauty, the struggle to adjust to being hard-up ...

Get out of the country, one friend had suggested: find a job abroad where you won't continually be reminded of Homewood Manor. Initially she had rejected the idea, and instead had taken a job in a solicitor's office after two months brushing up her secretarial skills (she had worked as a secretary before she had married). But that spring the weather had been appalling and sodden day had followed sodden day, making the work seem even more petty or sordid than it often was. Looking through the rain-streaked windows she had remembered how she and Gerry had put on shooting jackets and walked the fields, planning the sowing ... She had finally accepted the wisdom of her friend's advice and had handed in her notice on a Wednesday when the rain had turned to sleet.

She had decided for no particular reason to go to Mallorca. She knew nothing about the island, nor did she care what it was like provided only that it was totally different from England. On the plane an elderly couple had spoken to her and they had suggested she stay in Llueso.

Set about a hill and ringed by mountains, Llueso offered a sense of peace she had thought never to recapture. The locals called it a village, even though several thousand people lived there, and it was as a village that she loved it. There were very narrow, twisting streets, dozens of stores inefficiently run by women who preferred to gossip rather than to serve, a square where one could sit and drink and forget that there was a world beyond ...

She had been left with a small income, but she was not a woman who could ever be content to do nothing all day, every day. So she learned Castilian from a school teacher and Mallorquin from the people (she had not realised before that she had an aptitude for languages) and then applied for a job as a courier – one of the few jobs for which work permits were granted.

She was accepted, after a single interview, and regretfully moved down to the port because three of her hotels were there and there would be times when even the six kilometres between Llueso and Puerto Llueso would be rather too far to have to travel. It proved to be an arduous and at times infuriating job, but she enjoyed it because of the satisfaction she gained from meeting and helping a wide variety of people.

*

She went into the Hotel Pinos and crossed to the reception desk, to speak to the elder of the clerks. 'How is your wife today, Alfredo?' she asked in Spanish.

'The doctor says she is no longer in danger.' Relief smoothed out his round, plump face which for days had been sharp with fear.

'How wonderful! You must let me know when she comes back from the clinic so that I can visit her.'

'Of course, señora. Nothing would give her greater pleasure.'

'And how's the baby?'

'My mother is spoiling her most terribly. Every time he cries, she gives him something to eat: he has learned to cry a great deal.'

Right from the beginning she had got on well with the staff of the hotels, just as she had got on well with almost all Mallorquins. But then, unlike most of the foreigners, she had not made the mistake of believing that they were ignorant and uncouth just because their ways were different. 'Alfredo, I've come with a problem.' She put the blue folder she had been carrying on to the counter. 'I've just received the next lot of reservations from England and they've made them out as ten doubles and two singles for here. Didn't you tell me that you'd got down nine doubles and two singles?'

'One moment, señora, and I will check.' He went through the doorway behind the counter, to return in under the minute. 'That's right – nine doubles and two singles.'

'Blast!' she said in English. She switched back to Spanish. 'I suppose you're booked right up for the coming week?'

'Every room.'

'So what do I do now?'

He smiled. 'There will be some arranging, señora. There is absolutely no need to distress yourself. When your clients arrive, I will have ten double rooms awaiting them.'

'But how are you going to manage?'

He winked. 'Someone else will find she is a double room short.'

'But that's not really fair ... '

He interrupted her. 'The French señorita who is a courier is a very demanding lady, always complaining that we are incompetent. I will give her the pleasure of being right when I tell her that there has been a muddle and most unfortunately she is one double room short.'

She laughed.

'Lunch will be good today, so why not eat here, señora?'

She was entitled to eat at any of the hotels with which she worked. After a while the food they served became very monotonous, but there were times when she hated to eat on her own ... 'I'll do that. I've got to go along to the Meurice, but I'll come back here afterwards.'

'And I will speak to the chef and make certain he gives you two really good chops.'

'You're very sweet.'

'For you, señora, it is a pleasure.'

She loved the way they would suddenly become so formally polite and dignified.

Back outside the hotel she hesitated, then decided that there was time for a coffee. She crossed the road and went on to the hotel's terrace, which was built out over the sand and the sea.

A white-coated waiter, tall for a Mallorquin, came to the table. 'Good morning, señora.'

She chatted with him and then asked for a coffee. As she waited she watched a boy and girl in bathing costumes race along the jetty which stretched out into the bay from the terrace. It would have been wonderful if she and Gerry had had children ... But they hadn't ...

The waiter brought the coffee. She lit a cigarette and the air was so still that the smoke rose almost vertically. The heat closed in on her as she closed her eyes. Pray that there weren't too many complaints waiting for her at the Meurice. Miss, I don't like the food, it's not the same as what we get at home: I want to complain about two of the other guests because it's quite disgusting the way they are behaving – I am not a prude, you'll understand, but I was brought up to observe decent standards: Love, can you help my hubby? When he went swimming yesterday he opened his mouth too wide and lost his bottom set and just couldn't find 'em and now we've only my lowers between the two of us and it's taking ever so long to eat each meal 'cause we have to pass 'em backwards and forwards ...

She drank the coffee, then left and walked along the front, past shops which served the tourist trade and upgraded their prices accordingly, to the hotel Meurice. Modern, spread out because no building in the Puerto was allowed to be more than six storeys high, it catered for the cheaper end of the package-holiday market. She spoke to a couple who were sitting in the small garden, laughed at a joke she had heard twice the previous day, then went inside. The receptionist said that all was peaceful except for room sixty-four: the two occupants of that room had played football at two-thirty in the morning and woken up everyone in their corridor. Would she have a word with them – they were still in their room – and ask them not to do such a thing again.

She went up to room sixty-four. The two six-foot, thirteen stone twenty-one-year-olds, unshaven, bleary-eyed, were still in bed. They suggested she join them there. Briskly, but with unabated good humour, she turned the suggestion down on the grounds of age and then asked them not to wake up the hotel again the next time they felt like celebrating. They swore they'd be quieter than a couple of shadows. She doubted their promise even as she accepted it.

She left the hotel and, since there was still some time before lunch would be served at the Pinos, she wandered back along the front, for part of the time watching a windsurfer whose skill did not match his enthusiasm. She was about to cross the road when she saw Miriam, standing under the shade of one of the palm trees. Could anyone, she wondered, ever really mistake her for any nationality other than British? 'Hullo, Miriam. How are things?'

Miriam started, making it clear that she had not noticed Brenda. Her brows were drawn together in an expression of deep worry.

'I don't know about you, but it's become too hot for me. It wouldn't be nearly so bad if I didn't have to spend hours and hours at the infernal airport, waiting for planes. There was a three-hour delay last Friday and that was after ringing them before leaving here and being told the flight was on time.'

'You can't trust anyone,' Miriam said, her voice high. She moved restlessly and the sunlight, until then masked by a palm frond, struck her full on the face, causing her to squint.

'Is anything wrong?' Brenda asked, not from curiosity but because if there were trouble she might be able to help.

'Wrong?' Miriam repeated sharply. 'Why d'you ask?'

'I thought you seemed a little upset about something.'

'Of course I'm not.'

Brenda said goodbye and continued on her way to the hotel. Obviously something had been worrying Miriam, but she hadn't wanted to talk about it.

Chapter Five

Cosgrove, wearing shorts and sandals, stared for'd as his thirty-foot motor-cruiser rolled on the slight easterly swell. Gina was sunbathing, her discarded bikini by her side. 'It's drinking time,' he called.

She turned over and sat up. 'I'm going in for a swim first,' she said, in her slightly husky voice. She walked aft until she came to the break in the rope rails, balanced on the gunwale and then, beautiful body taut, dived into the sea. The water was clear and he watched her go down, trailing bubbles, before arcing back up to the surface. Her head speared the surface twenty feet from the boat. 'Come on in: it's lovely.'

'With all those stinging jellyfish around? Not likely.'

'Where? How close?' She began to thresh the water.

He laughed.

'Swine,' she shouted.

He left the flying bridge and went down the starboard ladder to the saloon. A tray with bottles, glasses, and an insulated ice bucket was on the table and he poured himself out a strong gin and tonic to which he added three cubes of ice.

When he'd lived in Besham Without, in that mean little semi-detached, hearing nothing but Rachael's moans and the kids' screams, he'd dreamed of life in the Mediterranean. For him, the dream had come true, even to a beautiful blonde swimming naked around his boat. He raised his glass. To dreams.

She climbed the rope ladder and stepped into the after well, came for'd and into the saloon. He hugged her, careless of the soaking he received, and ran his hand down her back, finally nipping hard.

'You really are a bastard – that hurt.' She rubbed her right buttock as she pushed herself free of him. 'Why do you like teasing and hurting people so much?'

'It's my sadistic nature.'

'Go and be sadistic with someone who likes that sort of thing ... Marie was saying last night that she thought you'd got a cruel face.'

'You should have brought her along today. She could have found out whether the nature fitted the appearance.'

'I'm not that daft.' Now there was a note of bitterness in her voice. She sat down. 'If I'd brought her along, you'd have been after her as well.'

'Nonsense. Have I never told you my motto? Never mix pleasure with pleasure.'

'Like hell. You'd mix anything with anything ... I want a drink.'

'What would you like?'

'Whisky.'

Of course, he thought. Whisky was the most expensive drink on the island. He poured out a large tot and added soda and ice. He handed her the glass. 'You've suddenly become scratchy. Relax. We're five miles out from land, it's a lovely day, and there's no chance of drinking the bar dry.'

'In other words, you're all right, so to hell with everyone else.'

'How did you guess?' She had lovely, long legs. Perhaps she wasn't lying when she said she'd been in ballet back in England.

She said abruptly: 'I'm in trouble.' She spoke with the sharp defiance of someone who was worried about how her words would be received.

He finished his drink.

'It's ... it's serious.'

He poured himself a second gin and tonic.

'You've got to help me, Blane.'

'What's happened?'

'I think I'm preggers,' she blurted out.

He stared at her in surprise and then laughed.

'What's so goddamn funny?'

'To get caught in this day and age ... Didn't your mother ever tell you how to keep the birds and the bees apart?'

She swore.

'Why the panic? Fly back home for an abortion and in a couple of days' time everything will be back to normal.'

'I can't.'

'Why not?'

'It's ... it's against my religion.' Her face reddened.

'Square the account with five Hail Marys.'

She was shocked by his blasphemous crudity. She stared at him for several seconds, then she said: 'I can't have a kid when I'm not married.'

'It's all the rage.'

'Don't you see, my friends will despise me.'

'Only for getting in a panic. Half the foreigners here are living in sin: the other half are too old.'

'But at least they're living together. That makes all the difference.'

'You mean, it cuts out the fun?'

'I mean, to what other people think.'

He finished his drink. 'You've given the romantic view an airing so now go for the realistic one. Square your conscience with the Almighty and I'll pay for the abortion.' 'Then you won't ... ' She stopped suddenly.

'If you've any ideas of moving in with me, forget 'em,' he said coldly.

'Whatever happens, I won't get an abortion.'

'That's your prerogative.'

'People will know the baby's yours ... '

'Correction. People will believe it could be mine. But if, sweetie, you're now trying to blackmail me into receiving you into my house, you're overlooking something. Despite all the bra-burning back home, in these expatriate parts there are still two standards. So as far as little bastards are concerned, the man's a gay old dog – in the old sense, I hasten to add – and the woman's a tart. It's tough, but it's fact.'

She began to cry and the tears spilled down her cheeks to fall on to the creamy brownness of her breasts.

He watched Gina walk down the short gangplank, her ridiculously high heels making it a potentially dangerous journey. When she reached the quay she continued towards the road without a backward glance.

He swore. Despite his confident words to her, he was worried. Back in Besham Without it hadn't mattered what happened because he had been a nobody. But here, because of his wealth and the fact that he could talk confidently about landed relations, he'd been accepted into society. He wined and dined with wealthy, important people, many of whom were ex-colonials who still prided themselves on showing an example to the natives. If they learned that he'd lowered himself to mess around with a woman who hadn't the background to know how to behave in a ladylike manner ...

He turned off the fuel lines, uncoupled the bottled gas, checked all ports, and locked all doors. He went ashore and pulled the gangplank on to the quayside, then crossed to his green Seat 132. Once behind the wheel, he tried to reassure himself. Give her a few days to think about the situation and then offer her five hundred on top of expenses to go back to England for an abortion. In this day and age, five hundred would surely buy anyone's religious scruples.

He drove down the quayside, past the boatyard and restaurant, and then along to the miniature roundabout and the Llueso road. The six-kilometre drive took him just on six minutes. He turned up past the football ground and continued to the dirt track which brought him to his house. As he came abreast of the twisted, ancient algarroba tree, around which the dry stone wall on his left had been shaped, he saw through the oleanders that a big Citroen was parked in his drive. He recognized it just before he saw Agnes, who was standing to the right of it, looking even lumpier than usual.

He drove past and into the integral garage, then returned outside.

'I've telephoned three times,' she said, belligerently. 'That damnfool woman of yours wouldn't say where you were.'

'She didn't know. And as a matter of fact, I've been out on my boat. Sorry you've had all this trouble ... Come on in and have a drink.' He led the way up the steps to the pillared portico, unlocked the front door, and waved her in. 'What will you have?'

'Something long and cool,' she answered, as she went through to the sitting-room.

He turned right into the kitchen, picked up two glasses, and went down into the cellar where he poured out two gin and tonics. He added ice from the refrigerator.

She took the glass and drank avidly. 'I've come to tell you something,' she said belligerently.

He raised an eyebrow in an ironic interrogation.

'I know where your land is.'

'My private El Dorado? I doubt it.'

'Cala Hispa.'

He lowered his glass. His expression was one of consternation.

'You're not quite as smart as you reckon!'

'And you, Agnes, aren't quite as accurate.' He'd regained much of his poise. 'All in all, I must have seen a dozen potential sites on the island, all of which were hopeless except for one. Cala Hispa was one of the eleven.' He shrugged his shoulders. 'A lovely situation, of course, because all the coastline round there is dramatic, but it's very small, the slopes are far too precipitous for building, and there's no chance of access.'

'Don't be ridiculous.'

'I assure you ... '

'And I assure you ... ' she repeated, mimicking his earnest tone. 'There's one thing you've never learned about young and beautiful women. If they get the chance they love to boast about their love-lives to older and not so beautiful women. I met Sonia yesterday and she told me all about that ever-so-wonderful picnic you took her on.'

'We went to Cala Hispa because I remembered how beautiful it was. There was no other reason for going back.'

'She can be a very boring young lady, but she didn't bore me yesterday for once.' Agnes's eyes were bright. 'She described the beach and the cove in great detail. It isn't very small, it's quite large: the surrounding slopes aren't precipitous, they're gentle: access isn't difficult, it's easy.'

'She was obviously talking about somewhere else. Knowing her, she was probably mixing up Cala Hispa with somewhere in Italy.'

'You don't give up easily, do you? I like a man who fights ... You parked less than a kilometre from the beach and most of the way there was a mule track which could be widened without any trouble at all.'

'It would cost a fortune,' he said indifferently.

'I got hold of a large scale map and checked and then rang my solicitor in Palma, who made some very quick enquiries this morning. Cala Hispa is in the Department of Santa Veronica, and for as long as anyone can remember the council there have been very left-wing. They've said several times that there will be no development of any land within their Department because land belongs to everyone ... They mean, of course, that it belongs to no one ... Cala Hispa is where you're aiming to buy if you can find the money.'

He hesitated, looked at her, then smiled ruefully. 'All right, I was a bloody fool when I took Sonia for a picnic. So now my secret is public knowledge.'

'Not public knowledge because what she knows won't have special meaning for anyone but me.' She raised her voice. 'I'm going to be your partner.'

'I told you ... '

'And I'm telling you, go on refusing and I'll make certain that everyone in Santa Veronica hears about the scheme. If the facts come out into the open, you'll never be able to bribe your way to being given development permission.'

'That sounds a bit like blackmail.'

'Call it what you like. If you'd had the sense to accept my original offer, there'd have been no need for it.'

'Publish and be damned.'

'Brave words. But I can read you like a book, Blane Cosgrove. You're not going to give up the chance to turn fifteen million into a couple of hundred million just to spite me. You've got the lust for money which keeps a man running.'

He finished his drink. 'I didn't realize you could be quite so sharp.'

She chuckled complacently.

Chapter Six

Alvarez, sitting under the shade of a fig tree, stared out over the parched field immediately in front of him to the irrigated one beyond. There, there was lush abundance – tomatoes, aubergines, peppers, beans, lettuces, chickpeas ...

A hoopoe, a splash of spotted colour, flew past in undulating curves: one dog barked and three or four others joined in: a long way away, a woman sang, her voice filled with the intonations of Arabia: bells tinkled to mark a flock of grazing sheep: the constant shrill of cicadas came from all directions. He sighed. Soon he must return to work in his stifling office. But not just yet ...

He awoke and now the morning was so hot that even within the shade of the fig tree the air was lifeless. He yawned, stretched, then stood and crossed to his car, which was under an evergreen oak. He'd left windows open, but even so it was like stepping into a sauna and by the time he had persuaded the engine to start his face, neck, and back were beaded with sweat.

In Llueso, he parked in the square, in one of the bays reserved for taxis, and then crossed to the Club Llueso. He went inside to the bar, ordered a coffee and a brandy, and sat down at one of the window tables. A waiter brought him his order and he drank a little brandy, then tipped the rest into the coffee, stirred, and sipped the coffee.

A guardia, passing the club, saw him and a moment later hurried into the bar. 'Man, half the world's looking for you.'

'Then now it can relax. I'm here.'

'You're supposed to be in your office.'

'When a man has been working hard since before the crack of dawn, he is entitled to a small break.'

'Not according to the captain.'

Alvarez gloomily finished the coffee.

'You'd better get back to your post smartly. Some foreigner has died down in the port and you're needed to sort things out.'

'If he's dead, there's no need to rush.'

The guardia left and after a while Alvarez followed him. When he arrived at the post, the duty guardia said: 'People have grown hoarse shouting for you. The captain's tearing his hair out.'

'More fool him: he's little enough to spare.' He continued along the corridor to the stairs and went up to his office. The shutters were closed, leaving the room in subdued light, and it was stifling hot: he switched on the fan, undid another button of his shirt, and settled down in the chair. He had just made himself comfortable when the internal phone rang.

'Where in the hell have you been all morning?' the captain demanded.

'Working, señor.'

'I've been trying to get hold of you since nine.'

'I was called to a farm up the Laraix valley, where a sow has gone missing.'

'Are you telling me you've spent all morning looking for some goddamn pig?'

'A pig, señor, is a very important animal to a farmer.'

'You're supposed to be a detective, not a swineherd ... There's been an accident down in the port – a woman fell from her apartment. A Señora Stewart is saying the accident isn't as straightforward as it appears to be. Doctor Maura was called and he saw the body where it fell. The dead woman's name is Señorita Spiller and the address is Almirante Vierna, number seven, apartment 5A ... And I want a full report as soon as possible.'

Sighing, Alvarez replaced the receiver. Of course the captain wanted a full report as soon as possible: his whole life was one long rush towards the grave.

The drive from Llueso to Puerto Llueso was one he always enjoyed. There were, it was true, a few houses, three or four warehouses, and the telephone exchange along the route, but otherwise the journey was through a countryside of almond and olive trees and vine-laden walls. Even the sight of the port, beginning to sprawl in ungainly fashion as the demand for housing overcame the objections of the conservationists, failed to dim his pleasure.

Calle Almirante Vierna, short and running at an angle to the bay, joined the Parelona road with the front road: along it were several tourist shops, two cafés, a restaurant whose prices made any Mallorquin whistle, three apartment blocks, and the side entrance to one of the larger hotels. He crossed to the lift. It was out of order. Resignedly, he climbed the four flights of stairs.

Short of breath and sweating heavily, he knocked on the door of apartment 5A. 'Inspector Alvarez, Cuerpo General de Policia,' he said to the Mallorquin woman who opened the door.

She was middle-aged, yet had the lined, drawn face of a much older woman: it was easy to guess that when young she had had to work beyond her strength. She looked at him with the wary and resentful stare of someone who clearly remembered the time when the police had had and had used too much power.

He asked her what had happened and she told him, her words rushing into each other. 'Señora, events are obviously complicated, so let's go through them more slowly.' He stepped into the small hall and shut the front door. 'Your name is ... ?'

'Ramis, Beatriz Ramis, señor. Do you wish to see my identity card? My handbag is in the kitchen and I'll go and get it.'

'There's no need for all that right now. But I'll tell you what, it's hotter than the Sahara and my throat's dryer than the sand. Is there any beer in the refrigerator?' 'Yes. But I can't offer it to you without permission ... '

'If the señorita were alive she would gladly give it, on compassionate grounds, so let's move along.'

She led the way into the kitchen, small but attractively tiled and very well equipped. She took a bottle of beer out of the door of the refrigerator and opened it and was about to pour the beer into a glass when he stopped her. 'There's no need to dirty that.' He took the bottle and drank from it, sighed with satisfaction. 'Now, señora, tell me about the señorita who has so sadly died and how it all happened.'

Made much more at ease by his friendly manner, she began for the second time, and far more rationally, to tell him the facts. The señorita was a dried-up woman who looked as if she had never enjoyed many of the pleasures of life. She had some money, but certainly wasn't nearly as wealthy as some of the foreigners, for whom a thousand-peseta note meant nothing.

This morning, as every morning, Beatriz had arrived at the flat at nine and had let herself in with her key. There had been no sign of the señorita, which was odd because, unlike other English people she had worked for, the señorita was usually not only up by nine, but had breakfasted. She had come into the kitchen and put on her apron, taken the vacuum cleaner from the cupboard, and had gone into the sitting-room. What a mess! In all the time she had worked for the señorita never had she seen such a mess. Newspapers and magazines strewn about the floor: empty tonic bottles by the bookcase: an ashtray knocked over so that the carpet was littered with ash and cigarette stubs: the record-player left open with a record on the turntable: a large stain on the cover of the settee where something had been spilled: the bottle of gin, usually kept in the cupboard for the señor, on the bookcase – where something wet had stood which had marked the wood she had spent so many hours polishing: the overturned glass which had left a slice of lemon and another stain over one of the chairs: the painting which had been knocked off the wall to fall to the ground so that the glass had splintered ... She'd wondered what on earth could have happened? Everyone knew that the English drank like fishes, but the señorita had never seemed to be like that. She had gone to the main bedroom and knocked on the door. No answer. She had opened the door. The bed had not been slept in. The french window, leading out onto the balcony, had been open ... Nearer the window, she had seen the bent balusters ... From the balcony she had looked down and there, by the dustbins, lay something which, Holy Mother of God, had seemed to be a body ...

'Why were you so certain it was her?'

She looked at him in amazement. 'But there was the open door out onto the balcony, the broken railings, and she was wearing the red dress which I had seen her in only the morning before.'

'So you immediately telephoned the police?'

'Señor, I swear it was as if the Lord had frozen my wits: I didn't know what to do. But then the front door bell rang and when I opened the door there was Señora Stewart. She phoned the police.'

'It seems she thinks it wasn't an accident?'

'She said the señorita could never have been so drunk as to go out on to the balcony and fall over and that's what she told the police. Then she said I must leave everything exactly as it was, which I have done, but I don't like this because when people come to pay their last respects they will think I have never kept the flat clean.'

'Do you know anything about Señora Stewart?'

'Not really, except that she works as a courier at the hotels.'

He put the now empty bottle of beer down on one of the working surfaces. 'Will you take me through now and show me the bedroom?'

It was not a large room, but because it faced north it was relatively cool. There was a single bed, with a quilted satin headboard, a large dressing-table on top of which were a number of silver toilet articles, a chair with hand embroidered seat, a brightly patterned carpet, and two paintings of local scenes. The built-in cupboard had louvred doors. The view through the large window was of dramatically shaped, stark mountain crests seen above an attractive patchwork of roofs with traditional variegated brown tiles.

'You seemed surprised that the french window was open, señora?'

'Indeed I was. She kept it locked always, ever since she found that the uprights had rusted ... However many times have I telephoned the builder and asked him to come here? But since when has a builder ever come when he said he would?'

He crossed to the open door. The balcony was about two metres long and one deep and the balusters were of elaborate design in wrought iron: the right-hand corner ones were bent over, trailing the rail with them.

'Be careful if you are going out on to it, señor,' she said urgently.

Having always had a paralysing fear of heights, he was determined to be exorbitantly careful. He stepped out on to the balcony. He imagined the moment when she had fallen against the rail and felt it begin to twist ... Sweet Mary, preserve me, he prayed, as he gripped the top rail. He looked down at the courtyard below ... A million kilometres below ... And saw the small concrete square, formed by the surrounding buildings, with several dustbins grouped close to one wall. He stepped back into the bedroom and with a shaking hand brushed the beads of sweat from his forehead. 'Have you any idea why no one heard the fall?'

She shrugged her shoulders. 'Who can say?'

Had the señorita been so drunk that she had not realized what was happening and therefore had not screamed? Had she screamed, but had not been heard?: there was a discotheque in the Parelona road, perhaps only a hundred metres from this flat. 'Did the señorita drink a lot?'

'She never seemed to, but perhaps she hid the empty bottles from me.'

'As far as you know, did she have many friends?'

'Very few. She was not a person to have many.'

'What about people visiting her here at night?'

'I can't say because I was never here. But only if her man had been here would there be more than the usual washing-up to do and then she'd tell me he'd been.'

'Her man?'

'She was engaged to marry him.' She sniffed.

'I shall obviously have to have a word with Señora Stewart. So in the meantime, this place must be left as it is and locked up.'

'But when you've seen it, surely I may clean it up?'

He shook his head. 'But rest calm. I'll make certain you have the chance to tidy it up before anyone else can see it ... Now, let's have a look at the sitting-room.'

If anything, the sitting-room was in more of a disorderly state than her description had suggested. He looked around and then said: 'There's the glass you told me about.' He pointed at the nearer armchair. 'Were there any others around? Maybe you took one or more through to the kitchen before realizing something was wrong?'

'I have taken nothing from this room.'

'And that bottle of gin?'

'She kept it always in the cupboard. Yesterday morning it was unopened.'

'Are you certain of that?'

'Quite certain.'

So now he had the picture of what had happened. The señorita drinking very heavily on her own: finally staggering along to her bedroom: needing fresh air on a night that was unusually hot and unlocking and opening the french window: in her drunkenness forgetting the state of the balusters and going to the end of the balcony and leaning against the rail: feeling the rail give and beginning to lose her balance, but reacting so slowly that she failed to save herself ... But for Señora Stewart, whoever she might be, this could have been dismissed as an accident ...

Chapter Seven

Finnister read through the two pages he had written that morning and he was struck by the sense of style and the profundity of thought. He heard the sound of high heels clacking on the creaking stairs and identified his caller as Carol several seconds before her head appeared above the level of the patio.

She had used too much make-up and her dress fitted too tightly. He would have pointed out those facts, but she engulfed him, kissed him passionately, and left him too breathless to comment.

'Frank, have you heard?'

'Have I heard what?'

'It's Miriam ... ' She held him tightly once more, offering him the comfort of physical contact. 'Frank, she's dead!'

'Don't be so ridiculous.'

'They told me in the supermarket. It's true. It's terrible. She fell out of her bedroom. Oh, Frank, I'm so sorry for you. I don't know what to do.' In contradiction of her words she led him over to the bed.

*

Agnes, who had just collected her mail from one of the post-boxes in the post office, stood by her car in the small side-street. 'Are you sure it's not just another of those rumours which are always going around?'

'I don't think so, dear lady,' said the retired colonel, whose career in the Indian army had conditioned him to women like Agnes. 'Apparently she fell from one of the balconies in her flat.'

'I must say that sounds like her: an extraordinarily clumsy woman.' Her voice sharpened. 'Damn and blast! Where am I going to find another secretary at short notice?'

*

Alvarez knocked on the door of the third floor flat in a block in the urbanizaciòn on the outskirts of the port. Brenda opened the door and he introduced himself. As he apologized for worrying her at a time when she must be saddened by the death of a friend, he tried to make out why her face seemed familiar, when he could be certain he had never met her

40

before. Then he realized that her eyes, brown, warm, filled with caring, were the eyes of Juana-Maria ...

'You'd better come in.'

He was surprised by the excellence of her Spanish: most English were too lazy or too embarrassed to try to speak it. Once inside, he said: 'I understand that the señorita was a close friend of yours?' She had a pleasant face, he decided; certainly not beautiful but filled with character. Her mouth even in repose looked poised to smile, yet in the lines about it he saw past suffering.

The sitting-room was also the dining-room, with the table near the door. Through the large window, which faced north, he saw the same view as he had seen from Miriam's flat, the mountains now a little closer and their crests become vaguely hostile. The furniture had the anonymous, battered look common to furniture in rented accommodation, with the one exception of a painting on the far wall which was not an abstract and yet was not representational and whose colours were bold, almost, but miraculously not quite, to the point of disharmony. He was certain the painting was hers.

'Will you have a drink? I can offer you most of the usual things.'

'A small brandy, señora, with a lot of ice would be very much appreciated.'

He watched her go over to the low cupboard and appreciated the grace with which she moved. His mother had once told him that one could always tell a 'good' girl by the way she walked. Experience had taught him that his mother had been far too optimistic, but even now one of the first things he noticed about a woman was the way she moved.

She brought out of the cupboard two bottles and put them on top, then added two crackled glasses in blue. 'I'll just get some ice from the kitchen.'

She returned with an insulated container. She poured brandy into one of the glasses. 'Soda?'

'No, thank you. But if I might have several ice cubes?' She crossed to hand him the glass, then returned to the cupboard. She left behind her the faint scent of wild herb-bushes in spring, when their heady, evocative perfumes were drawn by the first hot suns of the year.

She poured herself a vermouth and soda, sat opposite him. 'Now, you were asking me whether Miriam was a close friend. In one sense, we weren't really all that friendly at all. We didn't have much in common and we certainly didn't see each other every day, or anything like that. But in the sense that if she were unhappy and needed someone to talk to she knew she could always come and talk to me, then we were good friends. I hope you can understand?'

He showed his astonishment. 'But of course I can.'

'Well, it's just ... Some people never learn that friendship can be as much about helping as liking. And never about exploiting.'

He was astonished by the sudden note of bitterness in her voice. 'What kind of a person was the señorita?'

She sipped her drink. 'I'm not certain I can answer that because I never seemed to know more than the superficial her. She was very nervous, especially about foreigners – which is odd, since she chose to come and live here. She was very lonely. The wealthy people out here looked down on her because by their lights she'd neither background nor money and she looked down on the Bohemian set because she couldn't understand them. If that's making her out to be rather an unpleasant kind of a person, it's all wrong: she was a very nice person who just didn't fit in. Frankly, I think she probably spent most of her life not fitting in.'

'I am told that she had become engaged to be married?'

'A few months ago, to Frank Finnister.'

'And I understand that the señor lives on the island?'

'In the port, somewhere along the front. He's a writer. Not nearly as good as he believes himself, I'm afraid. He gave me a couple of his books to read and parts of them made me laugh – the trouble is, they're not supposed to be humorous. He takes himself very, very seriously.'

'Is he wealthy?'

'Far from it. In fact ... Look, I hate passing on gossip so does it really matter what he is?'

'I cannot say at the moment, señora. Now it is unimportant, but perhaps it will become very important. That is why I need to know.'

She hesitated, then said: 'Well, the very cruel story was going around that he was doing so badly at his writing that he had to marry her and face a fate worse than death, or starve.'

'Was the señorita fond of him?'

'She was looking forward to being married to him.'

'Is that not the same thing?'

She shook her head. 'In this case, probably not. I'm sure she had become ashamed of being a spinster and was desperate to bring an end to that shame ... I've made it sound rather twisted and melodramatic. It was really neither: just pathetic.'

'Señora, you telephoned the police and said there was something unusual about the accident. What caused you to say that?'

'As a matter of fact ... I was rather upset when I made that call. Anyone would have been. Beatriz was practically having hysterics, saying that Miriam must have been drunk to go out on to the balcony and fall over ... But Miriam couldn't have been drunk.'

'Why not?'

'She never drank much. You see, for her, it wasn't ladylike.'

'Yet the sitting-room was in the kind of state in which a drunken person often leaves a room.'

'I know. I saw it earlier on.'

'There was just the one glass so that it seems only one person had been drinking. And the bottle of gin was three parts empty, yet Beatriz assures me it was unopened in the morning.'

'She never drank gin,' she said flatly.

'Señora, it was quite definitely a bottle of gin.'

'Whenever she drank anything before a meal, it was sherry: sherry was respectable, gin was disreputable.'

'I don't think I understand that.'

'Unless you have ever been a British spinster, middle-aged and brought up in a certain type of household, you wouldn't. But I assure you that that's how she thought.'

'Beatriz said that she always kept the outside door in her bedroom locked because she was scared to go out on to the balcony. Did you know that?'

'Very much so. It was I who pointed out that the wrought iron uprights had rusted and looked dangerous.'

'Then would she have unlocked that door and gone out on to the balcony unless she had had too much to drink to think reasonably?'

After a while she shook her head to indicate that she did not know the answer.

'Señora, there are times when people do not behave as one expects. Perhaps last night the señorita learned something distressing: so distressing that all she could think of doing was to drink and try to forget? The señor, her fiancé, and she might have had a row ... ?'

'I know nothing about anything like that.'

He finished his drink, except for the small amount which politeness dictated he leave, and then he stood. 'Thank you, señora, for your help.'

'I hope ... I hope you find I'm wrong.'

*

He drove back to Llueso and parked outside his house at half past one. Dolores – they called each other cousin, but their relationship was not that close – was in the dining-room, talking angrily to Jaime, her husband. She was a striking woman, with the classical looks of an Andaluz rather than of the islander she was: an oval face, strongly and handsomely featured, jet-black hair grown long and drawn tightly back on her head, and very dark brown eyes.

'Listen, Enrique,' she said, as she put her hands on her hips. 'That disgusting man there ... ' She pointed at Jaime and paused for effect. Jaime winked at Alvarez as he poured out a brandy for him. 'That disgusting, worthless man says that this Sunday we are going to Parelona beach for the day.'

'What's so wrong with that?' asked Alvarez, surprised. 'The kids love it there. And what's more, it's safe for them.'

Her voice rose. 'And are you truly so simple that you believe he wants to go there so that his son and daughter may play on the sand and swim in a safe sea?'

'Why else?'

'Because some foul-mouthed man at work has told him that the foreign women are now so lost to all modesty as to display their bosoms.'

'Wishful thinking.'

'Neither would I believe such an impossibility. Not even a whore is shameless enough to display herself to all men. But Catalina's husband works at the Parelona Hotel and he says that it is indeed true, although God knows, it should be a lie.'

'What's wrong with a bit of sunbathing?' asked Jaime.

'You lover of filth. Do you then wish me to strip in front of other men ... '

'You can forget that idea or I'll knock some bloody sense into you.'

She stared at him, an expression of regal scorn on her face. 'That I am your wife is a misfortune, but it is that I am a Mallorquin which prevents me from behaving like foreign women.'

Chapter Eight

Alvarez awoke and the heat engulfed him, leaving him sweating and breathless. There was another thump on the door and Juan, now eleven, stepped into the room. 'You ought to have got up a long time ago, Uncle. Suppose I spray you with my new water-pistol?'

'I'll warm your behind until it bursts into flames.'

Juan aimed the pistol and then, giggling, left and slammed the door shut. Alvarez stared up at the ceiling. Juan and Isabel were growing up into a totally different world from the one into which he had been born. Men did not now have to get up in the dark in order to be in the fields at dawn where, if they were lucky, they would be given work which would earn them a few céntimos an hour: women did not weep tears of desperation as they tried to find enough food to feed their families while in the homes of the rich food was thrown away, because even gluttons could only eat so much ... But what values would Juan and Isabel hold?

He finally climbed off the bed and opened the shutters. The harsh afternoon sunshine made him blink and he hurriedly turned away. He yawned. Perhaps the only good thing about the future was that people would not be required to work so hard as they did now ...

When he looked into the kitchen, Dolores said: 'So you've overslept again! It's all that brandy you will drink.'

He turned and went over to the dining-room table and slumped down on one of the chairs.

She looked through the doorway. 'You look as though you're there for the rest of the day. You've no important work, then?'

He shrugged his shoulders. Who knew what would turn out to be important?

'Your coffee's ready.'

*

It was just after six when he finally left the house and drove through the narrow streets, past shuttered houses, to the guardia post. He went up to his room, sat behind the desk, and stared at the closed shutters. The phone rang. Where, demanded the captain, had he been all afternoon?

45

Investigating the death of the señorita down in the port, he replied stiffly: it was turning out to be a very complicated case. Then hadn't he better hand it over to someone else? asked the captain nastily, before ringing off.

After a while, he telephoned Maura.

'When I arrived,' said the doctor, in his precise, pedantic voice, 'the deceased was lying on the ground by the side of the dustbins. In my opinion, death was instantaneous.'

'What was the time when you first saw the body?'

'Just after nine-thirty.'

'Have you any idea when she died?'

'If by that you mean can I offer an accurate estimate of the time of death, the answer is no, I cannot. There was no suggestion that there was any need for me to make such an estimate. Why are you asking – wasn't it an accident?'

'At the moment, doctor, it's impossible to be certain. If it wasn't, the time of death is obviously going to be important.'

'I didn't take the temperature of the corpse – for the reasons I've just given – but I naturally noted the degree of rigor. It had commenced in the face and begun to affect the shoulders. Remembering the night temperature, that would suggest death took place between six and nine hours previously. But I must make it quite clear that at the very best, this is only a rough estimate. The onset, spread, and duration of rigor, are not open to certainty.'

'I understand that OK.' He pictured Maura with a frowning expression on his sharp, peaky face, annoyed because he liked everything to be exact. 'Were there any injuries which might not have been caused by the fall?'

'Your question is impossible to answer merely from a superficial examination and even a PM will probably not give a definite answer – unless you're suspecting something like a stab or a gunshot wound?'

'I don't think there was anything like that.'

After thanking the doctor, Alvarez replaced the receiver, then left the room and returned to his car, to drive down to the port. There, he went into a butcher's shop on the front and asked the woman behind the counter if she knew where the Englishman, Señor Finnister, lived? Five doors along, she answered, in the upstairs part of the house belonging to Señora Olmedo. Señora Olmedo, she added, as she battered the bone of a pork chop with unnecessary force, always pleaded poverty when she failed to pay her meat bills, but she charged the English señor at least four times the rent that that broken-down upstairs flat was worth ...

He thanked her and then walked along the road until he came to the creaky wooden stairs, which he climbed. He crossed the patio and knocked at the door.

There was a shout from inside. 'Come in. I'll be out in a minute.'

It was a long time since he had entered so squalid a room. The walls and ceiling needed repairing and redecorating, the floor wanted scrubbing: the bed wasn't made, there were books on the chairs and in collapsed piles on the floor, the remains of several meals were on the table, and a number of empty bottles were in the fireplace: a typewriter, overlaid by sheets of paper, was on a small table which had had one leg shored up with a wedge of newspaper, and more sheets of crumpled-up paper lay around the table.

Finnister came through the doorway which led to the kitchen and bathroom. When he saw Alvarez his surprise was obvious.

'Señor, I am very sorry to have to intrude at a time of such grief for you, but I am from the Cuerpo General de Policia and I regret that I must ask you certain questions.'

'It's about my residencia? Look, I know that just at the moment ... '

'Señor, I am not here because of that. I am here because of the tragic death of Señorita Spiller.'

'I thought ... You see, I've been ... ' He stopped, stared uneasily at Alvarez, then crossed the room, stepping around one of the many obstacles on the floor. He searched among the wine bottles on the table until he found one three-quarters full. 'You'll have some vino?'

'Thank you, but no.'

He picked up a dirty glass and filled it, trying to hide the extent to which his hand was shaking. 'About Miriam ... Why isn't the funeral tonight? It's always very quick out here, but when I asked they said it had been delayed. I can't understand it.'

'After such an accident as this, we have to try and find out how it happened.'

'But that's clear enough, even for ... I mean, that seems clear.'

'Señor, may I sit down?'

'Of course ... I'll move the things out of that chair.' He picked up a number of books from the single armchair and promptly let half of them fall to the floor. 'I've been working so hard there's not been time to clear up ... '

Alvarez sat, disturbing enough dust to make him sneeze repeatedly. Finnister looked round for somewhere to put the books and finally stacked them on top of others on a rush-bottomed chair.

'Señor, for how long had the balcony rails in the señorita's flat been dangerous?'

'For as long as I've been going there. I said to her, if the builder won't come and do the job, try another firm. But she wouldn't.'

'I believe she usually kept the door which leads out on to the balcony locked?'

'Always. She was scared of going out there.'

'Doesn't it seem strange, then, that in the middle of the night she went out on to it?'

Finnister stared at the floor, his face expressing weak uncertainty.

'At what time did she usually go to bed?'

'How can that possibly matter?'

'Please answer.'

It needed only a hint of authority to crumble any thought of resistance on Finnister's part. 'She always went to bed very early. And then because in the summer no one else turns in until very late, noise went on outside and she couldn't get to sleep and that made her so cross she got indigestion. I said to her, again and again, go to bed later, when things are much quieter. But she wouldn't. She was as stubborn as ... ' He suddenly looked at Alvarez with an expression of sharp worry. 'I suppose that ... sounds rather awful? I mean, criticizing her when she's only just dead.'

'When a man is badly shocked, he often says things he would not normally do.'

Finnister nodded, failing to appreciate that the words might have been spoken ironically.

'Did you see the señorita yesterday?'

'Only in the morning when she came to say she was going to be busy all evening so we couldn't see each other as we'd arranged.'

'You didn't go to her flat during the day?'

'I've just said not.' He suddenly worried that he might have sounded antagonistic. 'I mean, in effect I've just said that.'

'What did she mean when she said that she would be busy?'

'I don't really know. She did some secretarial work for an English woman so I suppose there was suddenly a lot extra to do in a hurry. Mustn't keep the high and mighty waiting,' he added bitterly.

'What did the señorita like to drink?'

'But what's that got to do with anything?' he asked plaintively.

Alvarez gave no answer and after a short while Finnister said: 'She never drank very much: wasn't that kind of a woman. In fact, she used to go on and on at me because she said that I drank too much, which I don't.'

'What did she like when she did have a drink?'

'Sherry. She'd been taught that that was a respectable drink.'

Almost the same words as Señora Stewart had used, thought Alvarez. What a strange race the English were! How could one drink possibly be more respectable than another? 'I imagine that she also liked gin?'

'She'd never touch it,' Finnister answered immediately.

'But perhaps just now and then she would have a little? If things became very difficult and she wished to be cheered up?'

'She wouldn't have touched it however she was feeling. According to her, gin was the drink of common people. If I told her once, I told her a dozen times that most of the old bores out here whom she used to look up to get plastered on it every night of the week, but she wouldn't believe me.'

Alvarez rubbed his heavy cheek. 'When I first came here you seemed very worried about your residencia. Are you perhaps having some trouble in having it renewed?'

'They've got all awkward about renewing it.' He finished the wine. 'It's not my fault.' Now his voice began to creak with self-pity. 'I can't help writing powerfully and radically. I'll tell you all that the publishers want – linear, repetitive mediocrity to fit the minds of the reading public. To hell with the public.'

'Are you explaining why there is trouble in renewing your residencia?'

'It's money. I don't bring enough into the country.'

'Señor, what exactly have you been told?'

'That unless I pay a couple of hundred thousand pesetas into my bank within the next three months, I'll have to leave the island.'

'Will that be possible?'

'She was going to lend it to me.'

'Señorita Spiller?'

'No one else out here would give a damn about saving me.'

Alvarez thought for a moment, then stood. 'Thank you, señor. Now I will leave you to get on with your work.'

Finnister looked up. 'Why ... why do you think she didn't just fall?'

'As I have said, as yet I think nothing. So I must ask questions to learn what happened.'

He left and walked over to the patio door and then outside. After the sordidness of the room behind him, the bay looked twice as beautiful: a brief expression of contentment crossed his face.

When he reached the foot of the stairs, an old woman, back bowed and face wrinkled by decades of sun and toil, shuffled out from the lower doorway. 'You're young, Enrique,' she said in Mallorquin, her voice distorted because she had no teeth.

'That's right. Only there aren't many who call me young any more.'

She laughed shrilly. 'You've the look of a man who can make a fool of himself, so you're still young. Your mother and I spent more hours together in the fields, killing ourselves with work, than I could ever count. Come on in and have a coñac.'

He followed her inside. The room they entered was bare of any furniture other than a rough, antique wooden chest, a sideboard on which were several framed photographs, a refrigerator, and a once brightly-coloured carpet, now dulled and badly worn: but everything, including the floor, which was composed of rounded pebbles set in cement, was clean and tidy. He felt proud that a peasant woman, such as his mother had been, could keep her home so spotlessly clean even when crippled by arthritis.

In the next room, into which they passed, there was much more furniture and this included a very large colour television set. He remembered that Señora Olmedo never paid her butcher's bills. Well, wasn't there a Mallorquin saying that the wise pig never grew fat ...

She poured out two large drinks and handed him a glass, then moved stiffly over to one of the chairs. The television was switched on and she had to raise her voice to overcome the sound of the commentary. 'So you've been up to see him.' She jerked a thumb in the direction of the ceiling. 'What kind of trouble is he in now? His residencia, or is it the woman who's just died?'

There was, he thought, no need to tell her any of the local news. 'He's in no trouble as far as I'm concerned: it's just that I have to check up on one or two facts concerning the señorita.'

'Did you ever meet her?'

He shook his head.

'There wasn't any juice left in her.' She looked slyly at him. 'Not like that other woman of his.'

'Other woman?'

'You don't know nothing about her ... And you the detective?' she jeered.

'I am not a very good one,' he answered contentedly.

She laughed shrilly. 'He thinks I don't know what goes on. But I've got eyes. And ears. I can hear when she goes up and when she comes down. And I can hear some of what goes on in between because she's a woman without shame.'

'Does she often come here?'

'Often enough to make me wonder whether maybe he isn't something of a man after all.'

'When was she last here?'

'This morning.'

'Impossible!'

'Haven't I just told you?'

'But with his fiancé just found dead ... How old is she?'

'Old enough to have a couple of kids, only she hasn't any because her husband's a drunkard.'

'Is he Mallorquin?'

'He's English,' she replied angrily. 'Since when has any islander been fool enough to drink so much that he doesn't know where his wife is and what she's doing?' 'What's her name?'

'How should I know? But she lives in Calle Pescadores and her house needs painting.'

'Is she pretty?'

'Listen to him – is she pretty? What weak fools you men are! Never mind if she can do a proper day's work and can cook and can avoid being swindled by the thieving rogues in the shops. Just "is she pretty?" '

Alvarez smiled. 'Judging from all that, she is!'

'She's like an October melon – over-ripe.'

Two women had fallen in love with Finnister. There must, thought Alvarez, be far more in the man than met the eye.

Chapter Nine

The solicitor s office in Palma, just off Jaime III, was luxuriously appointed with thick-pile carpets from wall to wall and really comfortable chairs. Forteza was in his late thirties, with all the smooth charm and self-confidence of a man who had had the sense to further his career by marrying a rich woman. He spoke in his rich, mellow voice to Agnes and Cosgrove, who sat in front of his highly polished, executive-sized desk. 'I hope the translation made some sort of sense?' His English was fluent and spoken with a slight drawl.

'It makes as much sense as any lawyer's work ever does,' she answered curtly.

He smiled. 'We dare not make things too straightforward or people will begin to wonder if we're really necessary.'

'A leading question,' said Cosgrove lightly.

'Indeed! ... Now, to the partnership agreement. There is a very considerable sum of money in question and even among friends ... ' He looked at them briefly. 'Even among the firmest friends it is much better to put down everything in writing so that later there can be no question as to what was agreed. I assume you have both read it right through? Has either of you any question on any point?'

'I've none,' she said.

'I haven't a question, but I do think there is one point I should bring up,' said Cosgrove, 'even though it's all been said before.'

'Better to repeat oneself twice than to deny oneself once ... Perhaps you will tell us what this point is, señor?'

'Put in its simplest terms, it's this: the sole aim and object of the partnership is to buy a tract of land and then try to obtain development permission for it, whereupon the land will be resold. This is a highly speculative venture and therefore inevitably carries the risk that there's a good chance of our losing all our money ... '

'You're not frightening me out of it, however much you try,' snapped Agnes.

'I'm not trying to frighten you, Agnes, merely to make certain you appreciate the extent of the risk.'

'For God's sake, man, allow me some intelligence. Of course I appreciate it.'

'In terms of hard cash? Look: the land at the moment is worth at the most two million pesetas. In order for us to buy it, we are going to have to spend about thirty million pesetas because the owner is fully aware of the potential and because we have to ... ' He smiled at Forteza, who smiled back. They both knew what had to be done. 'So if we fail to obtain development permission, the land reverts to being worth only two million and probably it would be difficult to sell. Are you prepared to lose your fifteen million?'

'Are you?' she snapped back.

'Yes.'

'That's not the answer, and you know it. You're not expecting to lose a peseta.'

Cosgrove shrugged his shoulders.

Forteza joined the tips of his fingers together as his hands rested on the top of the desk. 'It would seem, señor, that the señora fully understands and appreciates the risks involved. If she signs the agreement, she is agreeing to accept them.'

'Then I've no further point to make.'

'We are ready to sign?'

They nodded.

'I will call in my secretary, who will be a witness.'

Forteza's secretary was middle-aged, plain, and very efficient. She witnessed their signatures and then left the room with the agreement. Forteza said: 'May I be the first to wish you the very best of success.'

Agnes stood up. 'I want a copy of the agreement.'

'It will be in the post by midday tomorrow morning, señora.' Smiling, he came round the desk and shook hands with them, and only after they had left the room and he had closed the door behind them did his expression change. He wondered whether Cosgrove was just a man who was ready to take a risk in a business deal, or whether he possessed a much deeper character than was apparent.

*

The captain of the guardia post prodded his teeth with a wooden toothpick. 'So you've decided to call for a postmortem? Why?'

'I think I need to know whether the dead woman was very drunk when she died,' replied Alvarez.

'You think you need to know! Surely to God you're certain one way or the other?' Strictly speaking, the captain did not have any authority over Alvarez who, being CID, was a civil servant: but then, strictly speaking, Alvarez should not have worked from a guardia post.

'Señor, there are some cases where ... How shall I put it? Where a man does not quite know what he is facing.'

'A familiar feeling for you, no doubt,' sneered the captain.

'Let me try to explain what is here. A woman, no longer young and not pretty, went to bed early every night. Yet on the night of her death she was still in her clothes after midnight – why had she stayed up? There was a balcony outside her bedroom and the rails were rusty and she was very naturally afraid to go out on to it so always kept the door locked – in the middle of the night she went out on to the balcony, leant against the rails, and fell. Was she drunk? One morning she had a bottle of gin that was unopened, by the morning after her death it was three parts empty: in the sitting-room there was just one dirty glass, and many empty bottles of tonic – but she never drank gin, and her fiancé did not visit her within that time.'

'What's this fiancé like?'

'The kind of man for whom the world has always been too much. He writes books which do not sell and he has no money. The renewal of his residencia has been refused unless within the next three months he pays into his bank account two hundred thousand pesetas, brought from abroad. The señorita had promised to give him that money.'

'Then surely he wouldn't have given her the heave-ho?' Alvarez frowned. Death was always a tragedy and should never be treated lightly.

'If it wasn't him, who didn't like her?'

'It seems she knew very few people and was visited by almost no one. She was a lonely woman.'

'Who says?'

'The señora who was a friend.'

'You've just said she didn't have any.'

'I said she knew very few people ... Because of all these things, there needs to be a post-mortem.'

'More bloody paperwork.'

'And while I wait for the results, I will talk to the other people in the block and will find out if they heard anything, or saw anyone enter her apartment last night.'

'Are you saying you haven't already made those enquiries?'

'In an investigation like this, one has to move very carefully and therefore slowly.'

'If you got any slower, no one would know you were still alive.'

Alvarez stood. 'Señor, you come from Madrid and therefore cannot be expected to know the Mallorquin saying, "The hare goes faster but sees nothing, the tortoise goes slower but sees everything".'

'If it's a Mallorquin tortoise, it's still bloody hibernating.'

Alvarez left and went out into the street. It was the time of approaching twilight, when the extreme heat was over and it was pleasantly warm: when the narrow streets with their shuttered houses gathered about them a hint of mystery: when men and women carried out their chairs into the streets and gossiped, renewing their love of a life which moved slowly.

He came to the square. Here, there was no room for mystery. Very soon it would be the week-long festival of Llueso, and strings of lights had been hung above the level part of the square: the slightest movement of air sent them swaying, and when they were switched on their light, coming through the leaves, would cause shadows to dance across the ground and the tables. A small stand had been erected opposite the fish market and this was proving an irresistible attraction to children; the icecream and sweet stalls in front of the church were busy.

A voice broke into his thoughts. 'Hullo. It's an odd thing, isn't it, how once you've met a person for the first time you then never stop bumping into him again?'

He turned, to face Brenda. 'Señora, that is one of the pleasures of life.'

Her smile reminded him how Juana-Maria had smiled: immeasurable warmth, freely offered.

Her expression changed to become serious. 'I don't know whether I really ought to ask, but have you found out anything about Miriam's death? To tell the truth, I've spent all day wondering whether I should have talked as I did.'

'Why not?'

'Because I was so much surer of myself then than I should have been. I said Miriam never drank gin. But perhaps she drank it when she was on her own and there was no one around to see whether she was being "respectable". I said she'd never have gone out on to the balcony. But perhaps there were times when she stepped out on to it, almost hoping to fall ... ' She stopped.

'Why do you suggest that?'

'I'm sorry if it sounds ridiculous. But she was often so very unhappy. She was sensitive to slights and so many of the people out here are social bullies ... I'm sorry, I shouldn't be boring you like this.'

'Señora, you are not boring me and I wish to hear what you have to say. But would it not be much more pleasant to sit down and have a drink whilst you talk?'

They crossed to the steps and climbed them to the level part of the square. Many of the tables set out in front of the café to their right were occupied and one or two of the English waved a greeting at Brenda. Alvarez chose one of the outer tables, and a waiter came over.

'What would you like, señora?' Alvarez asked.

'May I have a sweet vermouth and soda?'

He ordered a brandy for himself. He offered cigarettes. 'I'm afraid these are Spanish, señora.'

'I prefer them. And can we stop being formal? My name's Brenda.'

'And mine is Enrique, señora.'

They both laughed. He flicked open a lighter.

She drew on the cigarette, then blew out the smoke which rose almost vertically in the motionless air. 'I was trying to explain something and not doing very well. The fact is, I've come to the conclusion I made a ghastly mistake in telling you there was something odd about the accident. After all, if it wasn't an accident ... ' She stopped.

'It either had to be suicide or murder,' he finished quietly.

'She would have been so desperately embarrassed to think her life was being pried into ... '

'Señora ... Brenda ... '

'Is it so difficult a name to say?'

He shook his head. How to explain that he suddenly feared saying it? 'I have to learn the truth and that is only discovered by listening to everything. You may be wrong in what you said, but you were very right to say it.'

The waiter brought their drinks and put the glasses on the table. Alvarez raised his. 'Happiness.'

'Happiness ... Miriam desperately needed that, but I don't believe she would have found it by marrying Frank. And I think there were times when she could recognize this, but tried not to.'

'Which is why you think she may have stepped out on to the balcony?'

She nodded. Her brown eyes held a distant look. 'One can be so unhappy one can be drawn towards death, never really knowing quite how serious one is ... I think you know that?'

'Yes,' he answered simply.

'I thought so. It's in your face.'

'And in yours.'

She drank, put the glass down on the table, fiddled with her cigarette, then said: 'I was married for eighteen years.'

'And your husband died?'

'Gerry committed suicide ... ' She was silent for a long time before she continued speaking. 'We lived in a house which had been in his family for generations, and there was happiness in every brick. The garden had a rose-bed which had been planted by Gerry's grandmother when she was a new bride. There was farmland and woods, and we knew every inch of them ... Gerry had a lifelong friend who imagined himself a whole lot cleverer than he was. This friend put a great deal of money into a business which was concerned with selling property abroad – on the Peninsula, in fact – and then there was severe financial trouble which meant that either a lot more capital had to be found or the business would fail. Gerry's friend was so certain that *he* could never have backed a loser that he promised to raise all the extra capital needed. He got an enormous bank loan, putting up everything he owned as security. Shortly afterwards, the stock market did one of its periodic hiccups and the quoted value of his holdings wasn't enough to back the loan and the bank said he had to increase his security. He was completely extended, so he came along to Gerry. Gerry had always held that the real test of friendship was how far one was prepared to help in trouble, and so he guaranteed his friend's loan without having any of the facts checked by accountants. By his standards, that would have been impugning his friend's honour.

Cutting a long and painful story short, the stock market stopped hiccuping and instead disappeared out of sight, and at the same time it turned out that the two partners running the business had been swindling their clients. What's more, Gerry's friend had originally guaranteed all partnership debts ... By the time it was over we'd lost practically everything. Gerry was desperate with remorse for what he'd done and he committed suicide. Most people saw that as the final weakness of a man who couldn't face life when the going became tough. I knew he killed himself out of strength: he loved life and therefore only by destroying his own could there be a big enough sacrifice on his part to make up for what he'd done to me.'

Alvarez said softly: 'It is sad that he could have been so wrong.'

'Yes, of course he was tragically wrong. His death merely made my grief almost unbearable. But he'd never learned the art of compromise, either with other people or himself. And he'd become so desperate that he wasn't able to think reasonably ... ' She broke off suddenly and shook her head. 'Damn it, why am I talking to you about all this? It's a private misery that's meant to be locked right out of sight ... It's odd, almost frightening, how this island seduces one into doing and saying things one would never say or do elsewhere. How long have I known you? Since this morning. Yet because on this island time is timeless I feel as if it had been for half a lifetime, which entitles me to bore you stiff with all my woes.'

'Is not a trouble shared, a trouble halved?'

'In other words, make someone else suffer as well!'

'You are very hard on yourself.' He drained his glass. 'There is something I need to know. The señorita was a lonely, sad person, but surely she must have had some friends? I need their names and there is no disloyalty in giving them to me.'

'I don't think you've quite got the picture yet. She had no friends. You see, she couldn't give, she was emotionally barren. It's understandable, even without knowing anything about her past life. She can't ever have been attractive, and it's terrible for a girl to look in a mirror and be quite certain that no boy is going to rush to say hullo. She was nervous and shy by nature, and far too ready to be deferential, which never helps even an attractive woman. She must just have become more and more withdrawn, resenting and being ashamed of her spinsterhood. And even when people did talk to her she was always suspicious that they were trying to make fun of her.'

He beckoned to a waiter.

'I don't want another drink, thanks.'

'For both of us, I think, tonight is a time to drink wisely.'

'A contradiction in terms? But you're probably right and I do need cheering up, so I'd love another vermouth, please.'

58

The waiter took the order and left.

The three loudspeakers on the front of the south face of the church, amid a festoon of wiring, suddenly played one of the tunes for the exhibition of Mallorquin folk dancing.

'That music reminds me of something I've been wanting to find out,' she said. 'Is the battle between the Moors and the Christians on this year?'

'But they fight it every year,' he answered, surprised.

'I've never managed to see them.'

'Then let me show you? I've friends with rooms above the route so that one does not have to be amongst the crowds.'

'But being with everyone else is part of the fun.'

He spoke doubtfully. 'I suppose if you really want, you could risk being crushed to death.'

She laughed.

*

Alvarez returned home. In the front room Isabel and Juan were watching the television, and he handed each of them a small plastic bag of boiled sweets. In the second room Jaime was seated, elbows on the table, and in front of him were a dirty plate, two glasses, a bottle of wine, and a bottle of brandy. He pushed the brandy across the table.

'Thanks, but I won't have one,' said Alvarez, as he sat. 'I'm not thirsty.'

'Since when has a man needed to be thirsty to have a drink?'

Dolores entered from the kitchen.

'Hey, Enrique's refused a drink!'

'Perhaps he is too hungry. It is now an hour since he should have eaten.'

'I'm sorry about being late,' said Alvarez, 'but because of the English woman being killed I've had to work half the night.'

'Have contempt for my cooking if you like, but please don't treat me as simple,' she snapped, before returning to the kitchen where she noisily moved things around.

'What's up with her?' asked Alvarez in a low voice.

'God knows!' replied Jaime.

Dolores returned with an earthenware cooking pot and a soup plate in which was a slice of oven-dried bread, and put them on the table. He lifted the lid of the cooking pot. 'Caldereta!' he exclaimed with pleasure.

'It will be ruined for having had to be kept for so long.'

'It smells absolutely delicious.' He ladled the fish soup on to the crisp bread. 'There's no one makes a caldereta like you.' He brought up a mussel with a spoon, scraped the flesh out, and ate: he sipped a spoonful of the liquid. 'Not even my mother ever cooked a better one than this.'

She could not contain her expression of pride. She watched him eat for several seconds, then said: 'The English can't cook soups. The women won't be bothered to stand in front of a hot stove to please their men. For them it's these packets of dried nothing.'

'Maybe that's why they all look like they've bad smells under their noses,' said Jaime.

She whirled round. 'Who asked for your ignorant opinion? We all know what you think of foreign women!' She walked to the kitchen door. 'Men!' she said furiously, before disappearing.

Alvarez topped and tailed a prawn with his fingers and pulled off the outer skin. He jerked his head in the direction of the kitchen. 'Something's certainly got her going. Had a row with her?'

'Not for a day or two. Forget it. Women love scenes: makes 'em feel important.'

Juan and Isabel came through from the front room. 'I'm hungry,' said Juan. He sat at the table and grabbed a piece of bread. He poured olive oil over it and sprinkled on some salt and took a large mouthful. 'Mama saw you when she went to Aunt Inéz, Uncle,' he said, his voice muffled by bread.

'Saw me where?'

'In the square, having drinks with a foreign woman. She said you'd be late for grub. And you were!'

Alvarez thought he now understood the reason for Dolores's anger.

Chapter Ten

In the block of apartments in Calle Almirante Vierna, Alvarez thanked the woman in 2B and returned to the landing. He used a handkerchief to wipe the sweat from his forehead, face, and neck. It was even hotter than it had been over the past few days.

He pressed the button to call the lift which, miraculously, was now working. What a morning! He'd spoken to English residents, French and English tourists, and Spaniards from the Peninsula, and no one had been able to help. Some of them had known Miriam by sight, but not to speak to, none of them had seen anyone enter her flat during Tuesday night or early Wednesday morning, none of them had heard anything suspicious.

The lift took him down to the first floor and he went over to the front door of the only flat on that floor and rang the bell. A woman, obviously very harassed, opened the door. From behind came the sound of a child crying. 'Yes?' she said in English.

'I am from the police, señora. I should like to ask you some questions.'

She sighed. 'I suppose you'd better come in. Sorry about the mess and the row, but ... Holiday! I'm telling you, straight, it's no bloody holiday for me, especially when my husband clears out because he can't stand the racket.' She led the way through the small hall into the sitting-room which contained a jumble of beach clothes, arm-bands, buckets and spades, and sand. A seven year old girl, face wet with tears, appeared and stared at Alvarez with wide-eyed curiosity.

'I told her,' said the woman, pointing at the child. 'Don't stay out in the sun or you'll get burned. She'll be all right, her father said, provided she's got plenty of cream on her. Didn't make any difference. The poor kid's as red as a lobster.'

'Señora, on this island we have a remedy which is very good. Mix together oil and vinegar and very carefully rub that on to the burns.'

'Oil and vinegar? But that's for salads.'

'And burned flesh.' Alvarez hunkered down on his heels to face the girl. 'Let's treat you like a piece of lettuce, shall we?'

Intrigued by his strange, heavy peasant face and his accented voice, she stopped crying and gravely regarded him. She asked him if he were a Red Indian and he said not really, but he probably had some Moorish blood in him if that was any good. In no time at all they were sitting on the settee, gravely discussing her doll which had had to be left at home and undoubtedly was feeling very lonely.

The woman sighed. 'It's the first time she's been calm since her back started hurting. You wouldn't like to stay here for the rest of the day, would you?'

'If I had no work to do, señora, there is nothing I would like better. It is wonderful to be with children.'

'If you can say that, you haven't got any ... Look, I know it's a cheek, but I can't get near her to put anything on her back without her taking off. D'you think ... ' she came to a stop.

'Señora, mix a little oil with the same amount of vinegar and I will put it on.' He spoke to the child. 'And because it is magic, the burning will stop immediately.' He gently used cotton wool to dab the mixture over the girl's back and legs. 'There we are. One, two, three, and hey presto ... All the burning has gone, hasn't it?'

She nodded.

'That is Mallorquin magic of the very best quality.' She put her hand in his and held it tightly. He looked across.

'Señora, I need to find out about the accident which happened to Señorita Spiller ... Did you meet her?'

'No. I didn't know anything about her until ... until she died.'

'I wonder if you heard anything during the night before last?'

'Heard anything?'

'Such as a scream?'

'I scream,' said the girl.

'I know. But please don't do it again because when you're a very old man like me it makes the ears hurt.'

'I won't scream again,' she assured him.

'I didn't hear any scream,' said her mother. She had been standing by an untidy pile of beach towels and now she suddenly bent down, picked them up, put them on the nearest chair, and began to fold them, as if she had to do something with her hands. 'But ... '

'But perhaps you heard something else?'

'I couldn't sleep because it was so hot. Then ... Didn't think much of it at the time. There was just this thump. Some drunk, I thought, and serve him right if he's a thick head in the morning. But it was quite a thump. Then I heard yesterday morning what had happened and I wondered ... Made me feel quite sick, it did.' She put the folded towels down on a small table. 'I mean, if what I heard was her ... ' She swallowed heavily.

'Can you say when this happened?'

'Just after one. I'd looked at my watch, thinking it must be much later, and then a couple of minutes or so after that there was this terrible thump ... '

'Señora,' he said, lying in order to ease her distress, 'it is most unlikely that what you heard was the señorita falling. The time is wrong.'

She plucked at the edge of one of the towels. 'Thank God for that! Ever since, I've been thinking ... Bert told me not to be so soft, but then he doesn't get upset like I do.'

He left the flat a little later, after promising the girl to call in and see her again if possible. He thought about driving to the solicitor's office, but regretfully decided that because he'd have to leave the car some way away it would be as quick, or quicker, to walk.

He had to wait for ten minutes and then Covas, with two English clients, came out of the inner office, shook hands with the couple at the outside door and assured them in fluent but accented English that they had nothing more to worry about and soon the deeds of their house would be completed, then saw them out. He closed the door and turned. 'So, Enrique!' He had a long, dark-skinned, pock-marked face with high cheekbones. 'It's a long time since we last saw each other. Come on in and tell me what's brought you.'

The office was neat and tidy, except for the top of the very large desk, which was awash with papers and files. Covas gestured at the desk as he sat. 'Look at it – work and more work! A man doesn't have time to live.'

'At least you'll have the consolation of dying rich.'

'With a wife who demands a flat in Palma and four children who do nothing but talk about skiing holidays in La Molina ... But you haven't come here to listen to me moaning.' He looked enquiringly at Alvarez.

In the old days, thought Alvarez sadly, when two old friends met after having not seen each other for months they talked at length about all that had happened to them and their families, but now there was no time for such natural civilities, only for business. The tourists' money had done far more than just ruin the coastline ... 'You'll have heard about the death of Señorita Spiller?'

'Indeed.' Covas leaned back in his chair, rested his elbows on the arms, and joined his fingertips together. 'Very sad,' he said formally.

'Was she a client of yours?'

He nodded.

'What work have you done for her?'

'I handled the buying of her flat and I drew up her will.'

'What d'you reckon the flat's worth now?'

'That's difficult to say. Prices of all property have risen so quickly it's impossible to keep up to date. She paid two million for it. It overlooks a busy road and hasn't a view of the sea, but it is on the top floor and there is a lift, and the workmanship isn't as shoddy as it would be if built now. I'd say it would fetch four million.'

'Has she any other property?'

'The flat was her only capital.'

'Who benefits by her will?'

Covas stood up and came round his desk to open the door into the reception area: he called to the receptionist to bring him Señorita Spiller's file.

When once more seated, he said: 'Then her death was not an accident?'

'I don't know yet.'

'But you suspect.' He leaned back in his chair.

'She was an awkward kind of person. I like to feel that I can create a rapport with my clients, even with the Germans who in business trust no one, not even themselves, but with her, ... There was nothing.'

'Perhaps she could see through you?'

Covas smiled thinly. 'The years haven't changed you, except to make you more cynical.'

The receptionist brought in a grey folder. Covas put on a pair of horn-rimmed glasses. 'Age does something else to all of us, Enrique. It slowly blinds, deafens, and weakens us until even a woman doesn't excite. Yet some fools say there are compensations. What can compensate for the loss of a man's virility? ... Ah, well, there's nothing one can do about it. Not even prayers restore youth.' He opened the folder and searched through the papers inside. 'Here we are.' He brought out a double sheet of paper and read quickly, then looked up at Alvarez over the tops of his spectacles which had slid part way down his nose. 'Everything she owns is left to Señor Finnister.'

Alvarez said slowly: 'That makes him a fortunate man at a very fortunate time.'

Covas closed the file. The phone buzzed and he lifted the receiver and listened. 'Very soon.' He replaced it. 'Is there anything more I can do to help?'

'Not for the moment, so I'll get from under your feet.' Alvarez stood.

'Come and see us all at home some time,' said Covas, not really meaning it.

*

At the second bank at which he inquired, the Caja de Ahorros y Monte de Piedad de Las Baleares on the south side of the small park-like square, one of the bank clerks told him that at the time of her death Miriam Spiller's account had had a credit of thirty-three thousand four hundred and six pesetas. And so far as he knew – which he cheerfully admitted wasn't very far – she had had no other accounts with other banks.

Alvarez left the square, walked down to the front and then along to Finnister's flat. He climbed the squeaky stairs up to the patio, oven-hot in the full sunshine.

'What d'you want now?' asked Finnister, not trying to sound welcoming.

'To ask you some more questions, señor.'

'It's a great help for my work, you know!' He hesitated and then, with the ill-temper of a weak man under stress, said: 'I suppose you'd better come on in.'

The room was, if anything, a shade untidier than it had been the day before.

'Well, what is it?' demanded Finnister.

'Señor, would you mind if I sat? It has been a very tiring day ... ' He went over to the one easy chair and sat.

'I have just seen Señor Covas.'

Finnister stared blankly at him.

'He was the señorita's lawyer.'

'Why d'you go to see him?'

'To inquire about the señorita's will. Do you know the contents of that?'

'Of course I don't.'

'Then you will not yet understand that you are her sole beneficiary?'

'You mean ... ' He stopped.

His expression became one of excited greed. Then he realized that in the circumstances this was hardly appropriate and he struggled to look mournful. 'Nothing can ever begin to compensate for her death.'

'Of course not, señor.'

He hesitated, ran his tongue around his lips, then said: 'I suppose there's no possibility that ... Well, that she made a later will than the one you're talking about?' 'Very little ... but the records in Madrid will be consulted, of course.'

'So it's almost certain ... ?'

'Yes.'

'It's a shock.'

'Is it, señor?'

He stared at Alvarez with growing consternation. 'You're not suggesting I knew what was in her will?'

'She might have discussed it with you.'

'I've told you, I'd no idea. She'd never have talked about her will: she thought well brought up people never talked about death.' A new and more disturbing thought occurred to him. 'You're not thinking ... ' He gulped. 'You're not thinking I knew about the will and so I ... '

'Killed her? Señor, at the moment I know for certain so little that I do not think anything.'

'But don't you understand, I couldn't have killed her?' His voice rose still higher. 'I'm not the sort of person who could ever do such a terrible thing.'

'I think that for any of us there are circumstances when we could kill: it's just that for most of us such circumstances luckily never arise ... You told me you'd been refused a renewal of your residencia unless you brought a large sum of money into Spain, did you not?'

'You've no right to go on and on asking me these vicious questions ... '

'I have every right.'

Finnister immediately backed down. 'I didn't mean ... All I was trying to say was that ... ' He came to a stop. 'How much was that amount?'

'Two ... two hundred thousand pesetas.'

'And the señorita was to give it to you? Where was she going to get so much money?'

'From a friend.'

'Who?'

'She never told me.'

'It would have to be someone quite rich, wouldn't it, who was a great friend? ... Yet it appears that she unfortunately had almost no friends and certainly none who were rich. Are you certain she ever really did promise to give you that money?'

'Oh, God!' he moaned.

Alvarez stood. 'Señor, in which house in Calle Pescadores does your friend live?'

Shock and fright loosened Finnister's face until he suddenly looked an old man. He shambled over to the table, picked up a half-bottle of wine, and drank from it.

'Will you please tell me which is the number?'

'Seven,' he croaked.

Alvarez left. He walked back to his car and then drove to Calle Pescadores. It was a road of houses, small and none of more than two floors, but with one exception all were well decorated and with colourful window-boxes. The one exception was number seven. The front door and the dosed shutters lacked most of their paint, and plaster had flaked off the wall: the single window-box contained only one geranium, struggling to survive almost total neglect.

Carol Davidson opened the door. The housecoat she was wearing was too small for her full figure and a seam had come unstitched down the right-hand side: one of her slippers had worn through at the big toe: her hair had not yet been brushed and combed: her face still bore the remains of the previous day's make-up. Yet Alvarez could look beyond the sluttishness and see the woman, and he saw a self-respect which had been deadened but perhaps not destroyed by bitter and prolonged unhappiness. 'Señora Davidson? My name is Inspector Alvarez of the Cuerpo General de Policia.'

She stared at him, a little uneasy, a little challengingly, then stepped aside. The entrance room was also the sitting-room. 'I've not had time ... ' She gestured with her right hand at the untidiness. Then she crossed and pushed open the shutters of the single window and let in sharp light.

'Is your husband in, señora?'

'Him? This is prime drinking time.' Her voice was scornful.

'Then if he is not in, I may speak?'

'What in the hell are you on about?'

'I have just come from seeing Señor Finnister.'

'Oh! That's it, is it?' Her shoulders sagged. 'When I heard what had happened to the old stick, I wondered ... All right, so no one's supposed to talk nasty about the dead, but she was a dried-up old stick when she was alive and she won't have changed by dying.'

'You did not like her?'

'She was as cold as a block of ice and I need people who are warm.'

'And also Señor Finnister was going to marry her?'

Her face hardened. 'All right, so it wasn't just because she was like she was that I couldn't stand her. It was also the thought of her marrying Frank. He needs all the warmth anyone can give him and marrying her would have frozen him to death. You see, Frank ... ' She stopped.

She walked over to the window. 'Life's a bloody joke, isn't it? I'm married to the biggest drunken heel in the port – and that's setting a standard! – but because I am married to him I don't want him learning about Frank and me.' She turned. 'You've got to understand something. I love Frank. And he needs me: to stand behind him and support him when the going gets tough, to help him climb out of his depressions, to tell him he's good when someone else has just told him he's lousy, to see he doesn't drink too much ... ' She suddenly seemed bewildered. 'For God's sake, what is this, a public confession?' She stubbed out her cigarette. 'Oh God, life can be so bloody cruel!'

'That is true. And it takes great courage to fight back. And you, señora, have great courage.'

She looked at him, searching for something which she finally found.

'Will you tell me, please, did Señor Finnister come here on Tuesday evening?'

'Come to this house? Don't you realize what Ted would do to him if he even so much as suspected?'

'Then did you visit him that night?'

'No.' Her voice became bitter. 'You see, I'm daft. I'll rush to Frank during the day, but I won't go to him at night ... a wife ought to be at her home, then. And also because I try to stop Ted drinking too much, even though I know nothing's ever going to do that. Have you ever heard before of anyone being so daft?'

'On this island, señora, we say that to be in love is to be touched by the March moon.'

Chapter Eleven

In Llueso, cocktail parties tended to be just as boring as in Sunningdale and perhaps the only essential difference lay in the proportion of guests who would become drunk. Agnes disliked going to such parties, but she enjoyed giving them because they enabled her to flaunt her wealth. Sides of smoked salmon could be flown in from Aberdeen, terrines of foie gras from Villamblard and, if she were feeling really bitchy, jars of beluga caviar from London (to remove any taint of communism or Ayatollahism).

In the summer she entertained around the pool and it had become traditional that before the end of the evening at least a couple of people would have been thrown into the water. Provided they were reasonably clean she didn't object because she enjoyed seeing people make fools of themselves. Her maids wore blue and white check uniforms and carried the bottles of Codorniu Extra with the labels uppermost so that no one could be under any illusions as to what he or she was drinking: from time to time the maids had their shapely bottoms nipped by the more amorous men, assaults which they suffered with dignity and an ever-increasing contempt for foreigners.

'Yes,' said Agnes, having drunk enough to be prepared to be hypocritical, 'it was very sad about Miriam.'

'Life can be so abrupt,' said the tall, imposing woman who disliked Agnes.

'It can be impossible,' said the tall woman's husband. 'What about the American market, Agnes? Lost a packet there, I'll bet.'

'One of my stockbrokers did advise me to go much deeper into it just before the dollar slid,' replied Agnes.

'And you dived in?'

She spoke with scorn. 'I sold out of dollars and went into yen and then back into sterling to catch that when it rose.'

'By Gad, you're a genius!'

She smiled complacently as she moved away. She was wearing a blonde wig which had been green-rinsed: her dress had cost forty-one thousand pesetas and it would have looked beautiful on a woman seventy pounds lighter and thirty years younger: the ruby, diamond, and emerald rings on her fingers, the pearls about her throat, and the diamonds on her bosom, glowed and sparkled with the warmth of fortunes.

She crossed the corner of the lawn to where Cosgrove was talking to a woman. Conscious that the other woman was younger, slim, and very beautiful, she ignored her. 'Blane, I want a word with you.'

'When?' he answered, with unfailing good humour.

'Later, after everyone else has gone.'

'Sorry, but Sue and I are just about to leave to go down to the port for dinner.'

'That'll have to wait.'

'I don't think I'm prepared to heed the royal summons tonight. I am rather hungry. Aren't you, Sue?'

'Absolutely starving, even though I have eaten rather a lot of the divine canapes which have been going around. I was saying to Blane just a moment ago, Mrs Newbolt, that it's been the most wonderful party I've been to since I came to this divine island.'

Agnes continued to ignore her.

Blane said: 'I could drop in tomorrow morning if it's important?'

'Of course it's important,' she snapped. 'You can come at ten-thirty.'

'I didn't know it was healthy to get up that early in the morning,' said Sue, and she giggled as she took hold of Cosgrove's hand in a proprietory manner.

Stupid bitch, thought Agnes, now thoroughly annoyed.

*

As Alvarez poured out coffee into a large cup, Dolores cut two slices of bread and spread olive oil and sobrasada over them to make a thick sandwich. 'There's your merienda,' she said.

'Thanks.'

She frowned, then turned and began to brush the perfectly clean floor. 'Do you know Jorge?' she asked abruptly.

'Jorge who?' He blew on the coffee to cool it.

'Jorge who married the English girl.'

'But of course I know him. Weren't we all at his christening and his first communion?'

'He told his mother the other day ... ' She stopped.

'Told her what?'

'That English women ... Well, they all shave under their arms. You know why, don't you? It's because they don't bother to keep clean by washing.'

'Are you being serious?'

'Didn't I see with my own two eyes only yesterday a foreign woman in the village wearing almost nothing and she had shaved under the arms.'

He chuckled.

'What's so funny about that?' she demanded angrily. 'It's the thought of you peering to see if she ever washed.'

'You know what's the matter with you? You just don't care any more.'

'Care about what, in the name of God?'

'Oh, Enrique!' Her voice was now mournful. 'If only your mother were alive ... But perhaps it is merciful for her that she is not. We bear you men in pain and with pain you then break our hearts.'

His astonishment increased. 'I'm not understanding a word you say.'

She looked at him with haughty compassion, then left the kitchen. He sipped the coffee. Had the man ever been born who could begin to understand the ways of a woman?

When he reached his office, he telephoned the Institute of Forensic Anatomy in Palma. A woman with a voice like a chair scraping across a tiled floor said: 'The professor has held the post-mortem, inspector, but not all the laboratory tests have yet been completed.'

'Did he discover any injuries inconsistent with a fall?'

'None, but he stresses that the physical damage suffered was so extensive that it is impossible to be conclusive on this point.'

'And the test for alcohol?'

'The deceased had a very low blood-alcohol level, well under point one per cent, and the professor is of the opinion that she had not consumed more than one large sherry, or its equivalent, in the six hours before her death.'

He tapped on the desk with his fingers. 'When will the other laboratory tests be finished?'

She became even more pedantic. 'That is quite impossible to say: such tests are not to be hurried.'

He thanked her and rang off. His rate of tapping became faster. Señorita Spiller had not been drunk – so what had happened to all that gin? What had persuaded her to unlock the french window in her bedroom and step out on to the balcony?

After a while he left the office and returned to his car. He drove down to the port, to find the place swarming with tourists, many of whom had arrived in tour buses. His temper was further impaired when it took him several minutes to find somewhere to park.

He entered No. 7 Almirante Vierna, took the lift up to the fifth floor, and unlocked the front door of 5A. The atmosphere inside was stale and oppressively close and he opened the shutters in the sitting-room and switched on the fan before walking to the main bedroom where he stared out through the window – unshuttered – at the balcony with the bent and twisted wrought-iron balusters. Could anything or anyone have persuaded her, if sober, voluntarily to unlock the door and go outside ... ?

He made a more thorough search of that bedroom and then of the second one. Nothing of the slightest interest. In a cupboard in the kitchen he found two bottles of sweet sherry, three of red wine, and one of whisky, but significantly no gin and no tonic water.

Back in the sitting-room, he looked round at the newspapers and magazines strewn about everywhere, the empty tonic bottles, the three-parts-empty bottle of gin, the ash and cigarette stubs on the carpet, the record player left open, the glass and slice of lemon on the chair, the painting with its glass broken ... Evidence of drunkenness? Or evidence designed to suggest drunkenness?

The empty tonic bottles and the gin bottle must be checked for prints. He collected up the cigarette stubs and spread them out on a low, black-topped coffee table. There were two brands, Celtas and 46: most people smoked only one brand. Celtas was one of the cheapest brands, 46 was fairly up-market. Beatriz would have emptied and cleaned all ash-trays in the morning ... As he stared down at the table, his attention was caught by something to the right of the nearer armchair. It turned out to be a lighter with a small crest in silver and blue enamel.

He telephoned the municipal police. 'Enrique here. I need a plumber.'

'You can always join the queue.'

'And I need him here inside the next hour.'

'You must be joking! If it's an emergency, you might just get someone along inside the next month.'

'Get hold of Domenech, wherever he is, and if he tries to argue tell him I'll start making enquiries into who's been selling all those smuggled Yankee cigarettes. He's to come to apartment 5A, Calle Almirante Vierna, seven. I want all the traps opened up and the water in them collected, so he'll need several plastic containers. Have you got that?'

'Who the hell's been putting a fire-cracker under your tail?' grumbled the other.

*

Carol reached the patio to find the window shutters closed and the curtain drawn across the door. Oh, Frank!, she said to herself, knowing a stab of pain at her disloyalty at such a thought, if only you could work a little harder ...

Finnister, snoring fitfully, lay on his back in bed. His pyjama trousers were frayed and grubby, his chin was heavily stubbled, his face was slack, and he smelled stale and dirty: she woke him with a kiss and then she hugged him to herself. 'I suppose you drank too much again? Frank, for God's sake, don't get like Ted. One of him's one too many. He's just a useless shambles, but you've your work. How are you going to write your masterpiece if you drink too much and spend all morning in bed?'

'No one will ever publish it,' he said bitterly, his voice muffled because his face was pressed against her breasts.

'Don't talk like that. You've got to fight; the whole of this bloody life is a fight. Look, you get up and wash and shave, and I'll cook your breakfast, and when that's inside you, you can start writing.'

'I'm not in the mood today.'

'Then you'd better change moods.' She released him and crossed to the window to throw open the shutters. 'Look at it. Not a cloud in the sky and the sea's like a warm bath. People pay hundreds of quid to come out here and look at the bay and here you are, still in bed. Get a move on.'

'I've a bit of a head ... '

'If you're not off that bed in five seconds flat, love, you'll have a bit of a something else as well.'

Groaning, he came to his feet. 'You don't understand. A writer can't just chum out the words. He needs inspiration ... '

'Which he doesn't find snoring his head off in the middle of the morning.'

'De Quincey ... '

'Bugger de Quincey!'

He slouched through to the bathroom and she went into the kitchen. Clearly he had done no washing-up in days. 'Frank,' she murmured, 'you're not fit to be on your own.' She put as many plates and cutlery as

73

possible in to soak, then made coffee and fried two eggs, two rashers of bacon, three cloves of garlic in their skins, and a slice of bread.

When she carried the breakfast through on a tray, she found him looking almost neat, standing in front of the fireplace. 'There you are, love. Get that down inside you and the inspiration'll flow faster than a brandy into Ted's belly.'

'I've something to tell you ... '

'And I've something to tell you. I've not gone to all the trouble of cooking this for you to stand around and watch it get cold and gooey. So come on and eat.'

He left the fireplace, walked over to the table, and sat. She pushed some of the mess to one side to make enough room for the plate and cup. 'I hope the eggs are just as you like 'em?'

He cut the yolk of one with a knife. 'You've done them a bit much.'

'Oh, well, as my sister Eileen said about her husband, better to be done too much than too little, 'cause then you only start wondering what he's up to.' She rested her hand on his shoulder. Peter Pan had never grown up, either.

He finished eating, drank the coffee, and lit a cigarette.

'That detective was here again ... '

'He came and saw me too,' she broke in, and she removed her hand. 'Looks a bit odd and like he could get really bloody-minded if he wanted to, but I'd say he's real nice inside.'

'What did he want with you?'

'He was asking about Tuesday night: whether I'd been here or you'd been to my place.'

'What did you tell him?'

'That I hadn't seen you, of course: what d'you expect me to say?'

'Why didn't you ... ?' He cleared his throat. 'He came here to tell me that Miriam's left me everything she possessed.'

She stared at him, wide-eyed. 'Everything?' she whispered.

He nodded.

'The flat?'

He nodded again.

'You're going to have somewhere decent to live, instead of this dump? So the guardia won't go for you any more, and you'll be given a residencia and be able to stay on the island ... Oh, my darling! It's like some fairy's suddenly waved a wand. I've spent days and nights with the nightmare of you being forced to leave the island and me being forced to stay here and it's been like slowly freezing to death. But now ... Frank, oh Frank!' She grabbed him to her again.

'You don't understand the terrible implications,' he said fretfully, after disengaging his head. 'He thinks she may have been murdered. And my inheriting her estate gives me a motive. He suspects me of killing her!'

'You kill someone? That's being dafter than even my aunt Meg ever was.' She began to stroke his cheek.

*

Cosgrove drove through the gateway of Ca'n Blat. People who'd known the gardens before Agnes had bought the house, he thought, said how beautifully informal it had been then and how vulgarly formal it was now. Probably. Yet on this island nature was prodigal, and when one saw the huge banks of colour set off by the very large lawn – and of necessity few people had even a pocket-handkerchief-sized one – it was possible to realize that there could be merit in vulgarity. Then, as he parked, Agnes, a cream-shot bouffant brunette, came out of the house and he amended his thoughts: there could be merit in vulgarity where nature was concerned, but not where humans were.

She greeted him by saying petulantly: 'You said you'd be here at ten-thirty.'

'Not so. You told me I could be here at ten-thirty, I gave no definite time for my arrival.' He smiled.

She muttered something, turned and led the way round the side of the house, past oleander bushes, to the patio which was shaded by vines whose grapes hung down in large bunches.

There were several patio chairs set around two glass-topped tables and she sat at the nearer one. 'Ring the bell,' she said in a peremptory tone, pointing to the bell-push in the wall of the house.

He rang the bell and then sat and stared past the edge of the overhead vines at the mountains, whose lower slopes were dotted haphazardly with trees, but whose upper slopes were mainly stark and bare and coldly beautiful. He expected Agnes to speak, but she said nothing until a maid came from inside out on to the patio.

'I want coffee and some cake,' said Agnes, in English. She understood enough Castilian to be able to detect insolence in her staff, but would never speak it because this might have given them a chance to laugh at her mistakes.

As the maid returned into the house, Agnes said sharply:

'I want to know what's happening. Have you bought the land?'

He answered casually: 'No, not yet.'

'Why not?'

'Because out here, amongst the fiercest traders this side of Beirut, one daren't rush things. If I'd gone to the owner and said here's the money, give me the deeds to the land, he'd have wondered about my haste. He'd have come to the conclusion he was missing out on something and would then have told me there was suddenly a slight hitch and his wife's fourth cousin who owns one twentieth share in the land wouldn't agree to sell ... '

'There's no need to lecture me on how to bargain.'

'Is that what it sounded like? I'm sorry. I'll cut the story short. What I've done so far is to reopen the bargaining and try to drive down the agreed price. The owner now respects me for my immorality in not honouring the contract we've already agreed and when he finally forces me to pay the original price he'll be so chuffed with himself that he'll grab the money without a second thought.'

'Leave it too long and someone else may step in and buy it from under our noses.'

'Not a chance.'

'You can't be certain.'

He didn't bother to answer.

The maid returned with a silver tray on which were silver coffee and cream jugs, silver sugar bowl, two cups and saucers, two silver dessert forks, and two large slices of strawberry layer-cake, smothered with whipped cream, on plates. She set everything out on the table and poured the coffee.

Agnes used a fork to cut off a large piece of cake, well topped with cream. Her cheeks bulged as she ate. Cosgrove laughed to himself.

The plumber was a small man with a very dark complexion. As he stepped into the flat, he said belligerently to Alvarez: 'I've never sold a pack of smuggled cigarettes in my life.'

'Then the next man who assures me I can buy from you at half-price I'll call a liar.'

The plumber looked a shade sourer.

'What I want is for you to open each trap in the place and to drain them into separate containers and label which came from where.'

The plumber's curiosity became greater than his sense of resentment. 'What are you looking for?'

'Gin.'

'If they don't know a better way of getting rid of gin than pouring it down the sink, these foreigners must be even dafter than I thought.'

Chapter Twelve

Alvarez returned to the street, carrying a carrier bag in which were five plastic containers filled with scummy liquid. He went along to where his car was parked, between the two arms of the harbour, and put the carrier bag on the back seat, looked at his watch, and then left and crossed the road to the Hotel Pinos. The receptionist said that Señora Stewart had left there about a quarter of an hour ago and so far as he knew she had gone to the Hotel Bahia Azul.

The walk took him along a footpath, which continued round at the water's edge after the road had turned inland, past large, relatively old houses set in palm-studded gardens, now worth so much money that it made a man blink to think about it.

The Hotel Bahia Azul, built since the tourist boom and recently extended, catered for the package tourist trade, yet managed to keep its standards fairly high. He turned off the footpath and entered, and immediately heard an Englishman talking loudly and belligerently.

The Englishman was standing in front of the reception desk. He was in his middle twenties, ginger-haired, unshaven, dressed in a dirt-stained T-shirt and only slightly less dirty cotton trousers. He slammed his right fist down on the counter. 'I'm telling you, I didn't buy them bloody drinks.' By his side was a younger, slighter man, clearly nervous, and beyond them stood Brenda, her expression very worried. There were two reception clerks behind the desk and as Alvarez approached the assistant manager, formally dressed despite the heat, came out of the office.

'Señor,' said the assistant manager, 'I believe there to be some trouble?'

'You can say that again! I'm leaving this afternoon and your blokes have just tried to give me a bill for fifteen thousand bloody pesetas ... D'you know what you can do with the bill? You can shove it!'

The assistant manager spoke quickly in Mallorquin to the two receptionists, then turned and said in English: 'Señor, you have been drinking much since you stay here.' 'I've had a drink, or two, dead right, but not fifteen thousand pesetas' worth.'

'Mr James,' said Brenda, 'you must remember that you had a party last night out on the patio ... '

'Party? There weren't no party. Me and some pals had a drink, or two, that's all.'

'But the waiters have said that you were out on the patio for a long time and you were inviting everyone to have drinks. You've seen all the chits you signed ... ' 'They're bloody forgeries.'

'They really aren't. Perhaps you don't remember very clearly ... '

'If you're trying to say I was tight, forget it. I know the way that swindle works. This bunch of crooks frig me for fifteen thousand and you get a share. Well, I've news for you. I've met your kind of bitch before ... '

Alvarez stepped forward. 'Señor.'

They all turned and stared at him.

'Well?' said James belligerently.

'Señor, in this country we do not speak to a lady in such a way.'

'I'll speak to her how I bloody like, mate, without reference to some broken-down git like you.'

'Alf, cool it,' said the second Englishman urgently. James stared down at Alvarez with contempt. 'I've been around, see. And I know the rackets. I have a drink or two, and ask my pals to have a drink or two, and the management tries to take me for a sucker. Then if I don't fold easy and kick up a bit of a row, the courier starts standing by the management. Bitches like her ... '

Alvarez hit him in the stomach. The blow did not travel very far, but he doubled up, giving a whimpering woof of sound as he did so. At a quick command from the assistant manager, the two receptionists came round the counter and, supporting James on either side, led him into the small office so that he was out of sight of other guests.

The second Englishman said wildly: 'You didn't have no call to do that.'

'Señor,' replied Alvarez, 'I tried to explain to your friend, but he would not understand. In this country, we do not insult a lady.'

The Englishman, voice now shrill, said to the assistant manager: 'Call the police.'

'Señor Alvarez is of the police,' replied the assistant manager unemotionally.

James came staggering out of the office, his face white and strained. 'I'm going to get you for that,' he shouted at Alvarez.

'Don't,' cried his companion, 'he's a copper.'

'A ... a copper?' James gripped the counter for support. 'But he hit me!'

'Señor,' said Alvarez, 'in this country if a policeman is threatened he is not obliged to suffer a serious injury before he may defend himself. Also, to hit a policeman is a very serious offence, so when I understood you were expecting to return to England today it was necessary for me to make certain that you were not violent or I should be compelled to arrest you. That is why I helped you.'

'Helped me? By slugging me in the guts and near killing me when I hadn't done a bloody thing?'

'You should not have raised your fist, señor.'

'I didn't.'

'On the contrary, we all saw you do it.' Alvarez indicated the assistant manager and the two reception clerks. They nodded.

James was bewildered and also scared suddenly to discover that he was in a country where an individual did not have a right loutishly to make a nuisance of himself.

'There is your bill to pay, señor,' said the assistant manager politely.

James hesitated. Then, flinching with the movement, he reached back to the hip pocket of his trousers and brought out a bundle of notes and began to count them.

Alvarez said to Brenda: 'Señora, will you be kind enough to come with me so that I may ask you a few questions?'

Watched by James, still as much bewildered as resentful, Alvarez led the way out of the hotel and across the footpath to the patio, which stretched out over the sea. They sat at an outside table: by looking over the side they could see in the crystal-clear water the dozens of grey mullet who were regularly fed by hotel guests.

'I wish you hadn't done that,' she said. 'I've become used to being called all sorts of names. It's just part of the job and it doesn't mean nearly as much in England as it does in Spain.'

'We are in Spain, not England.'

'Surely you can't expect people like that man to realize the fact?'

'I think that now he realizes it.'

She looked away from him and out at the bay. 'Enrique, if there's violence over so unimportant a matter, what terrible things can happen when the matter's important?'

'A woman's honour is never unimportant.'

She sighed. 'I suppose no foreigner can ever understand the true character of you islanders. But maybe I've just discovered why people normally so kind can all of a sudden be so hard and cruel. It's because emotionally you're still living in the past: each of you a Don Quixote tilting at the windmills of reality. All right, now the young here are just as familiar with the horrors of the plastic society as they are in England, but the older people ... You're all so proud you can't begin to compromise and adapt.'

'Without pride, a man is nothing.'

'With pride, he's too much.'

'Brenda, had my mother, my sister, or my wife, been called a bitch, I would have acted immediately: so would every other man who truly is a man.'

'All right, I get the message. Instead of lecturing you, I ought to be thanking you as any Spanish lady would. Only I hate violence and it made me feel sick to see the man in such pain.'

The waiter came up to their table and they gave their orders.

'You said you wanted to ask me some questions?' she reminded him, bringing to an end their previous conversation.

He wondered if she knew how, when she spoke earnestly, she held her head high, like a woman of much pride? 'I need to understand more about Señorita Spiller.'

'But I really have told you all I can. Wouldn't it pay you better to have a word with Frank Finnister?'

'I have already spoken to him.'

'Oh!' She hesitated, then said: 'Are you certain now whether or not it was an accident?'

'No, but I think I soon shall be.'

She could judge what he expected the answer to be. 'It's ... it's a horrible thought that perhaps she was murdered.'

'That is why I need to uncover the truth as quickly as possible. The señorita bought the apartment in which she lived. Do you know where that money came from?'

'I've no idea.'

'Here on the island I am told she worked for an English señora called Newbolt. Can you tell me what kind of a woman she is and if she is rich?'

'She's rich, all right. As to what kind of a woman? The kind who makes me want to apologize to everyone for being English.'

81

The waiter returned and put two glasses on the table. She continued: 'I'll bet no other country produces the species, except perhaps America. Vulgar, thoughtless, intolerant, measuring everything and everybody solely by material worth, despising anyone poorer than herself ... Does that make me sound really bitchy – if I'm allowed to use the word about myself? I don't mind people being rich: it's when they start thinking that money makes them superior that I get hot under the collar.'

'Perhaps it was she who was going to give the señorita the large sum of money to give to Señor Finnister?'

'She wouldn't give a farthing to a blind beggar unless she thought she'd make on the deal.'

He raised his glass. 'Happiness.'

'I've never heard anyone else say that, but I like it so much more than the usual greetings. "Happiness!"' She drank. 'I'm afraid I mustn't be too long before I get back to work, Enrique.'

'We have only just sat down.'

'I know, but tourists have an amazing knack of getting into trouble and it's my job to get them out of it.'

'For once, let them find their own way.'

'Maybe I'd be tempted to, if I didn't have a boss who sometimes checks up on whether I'm doing my job.'

'If he annoys you, I will speak to him.'

'That could be disastrous! He's a blunt Yorkshireman and he might let his tongue run away with him. I hate to think how you'd react!'

He smiled.

'You realize, don't you,' she went on, 'that you've just denied your whole upbringing? – you've laughed at a question of honour.'

'Perhaps I am slowly learning to compromise.'

She turned sideways, to look out at the bay.

He cleared his throat, then said: 'There is a display of Mallorquin country dancing in the square in Llueso tonight.'

'Is there?' she said off-handedly.

'And when that is finished there will be dancing for everyone with the local band and a group. The bars will not shut for three days or nights.'

'I'm glad I'm living down here, in the port.'

'You told me you were interested in folk dancing. Would you like to watch it with me?'

After a while, she answered: 'I'm afraid I have to take one bus load to the airport and bring another one out tonight.'

'At what time will you return?'

'We're due to be here at eight: but none of the planes are arriving on time these days.'

'The display of folk dancing does not start until ten-thirty.'

'I have to see the people to their various hotels and sort out all their problems. If there's a mix-up with the rooms it can take me hours before I get everyone happy.'

'But if there is no trouble?'

She turned and faced him and spoke bluntly. 'Are you sure it's wise?'

'At our age surely everything is wise if it gives pleasure and no pain?'

'Maybe ... I'd love to go with you.'

By the happy Lord, he thought, it was a glorious day.

*

Finnister was working at his typewriter when Alvarez approached across the outside patio.

'Señor, I much regret disturbing you yet again, but it is necessary.' He took from his pocket the lighter he had found in the flat. 'Do you know who owns this?' He held it out.

Finnister took it. 'I most certainly do. It's mine and I've been looking for it for days. Where on earth did you find it?'

'In the señorita's flat. May I now have it back, please?'

'It's mine. This crest is ... '

'Señor, for a little I must keep it.'

Finnister hesitated, then with the exaggerated gestures of a petulant boy he passed it back.

'Thank you ... Will you now please tell me what brand of cigarettes the señorita smoked?'

'What the hell? ... Forty-six.'

'And you – what brand do you smoke?'

'Celtas. I can't afford anything better.'

'Did you go to the señorita's flat at any time on Tuesday?'

'Haven't I answered that a dozen times already? I didn't go near the place.'

'Then can you explain to me how your lighter reached her flat on Tuesday?'

'Who says it did?'

'I found it there.'

'All right, so I lost it there, but not on Tuesday.'

'Beatriz, the señorita's maid, cleaned the flat on Tuesday morning and the lighter was not by the chair. On Wednesday morning it was there. She also says that when she left the flat on Tuesday all the ash-trays were clean. Yet the next morning some of them contained the stubs of Celtas cigarettes as well as those of Forty-six.'

'You're ... you're not trying to suggest ... '

'Señor, it begins to be more and more likely that the señorita was murdered. So I have to ask myself, who had a reason for murdering her?'

'I swear I didn't go near her flat.'

'Then I have now asked all the questions I wish.' He dropped the lighter into his trouser pocket. 'I will leave and you may continue to write your book.'

'How in the hell can I write anything when you've as good as accused me of murdering her?' he demanded plaintively.

Chapter Thirteen

Alvarez parked the car and entered the house. 'Who's that?' Dolores called out.

'It's me.' He went through the front room into the second room and stood in front of the fan, which was switched on.

Dolores entered from the kitchen. 'I'm glad you're back early ... Aren't you going to pour yourself a drink?'

He was surprised by the encouragement. 'Will you have one?' he asked, as he crossed over to the sideboard and brought out a bottle of brandy and two glasses.

'I don't know – I've a lot of cooking still to do. But maybe just a very small one, then.'

He poured out the drinks. 'What's for supper?'

'Chick peas in garlic sauce, savoury rice, and then loin of pork.'

He passed her a glass. 'It sounds like Christmas!'

'Well, as a matter of fact ... ' She looked very quickly at him. 'Someone's coming to the meal.'

He sat in one of the easy chairs beyond the table, stretched out his legs, and drank.

'Teresa Benmasar is having dinner with us.'

'But I thought you didn't get on well with her?'

'Things change,' she replied vaguely.

'Didn't her man die not long back?'

'No more than ten months ago. It was tragic: one moment he was alive, the next he was dead ... She's a good widow. Every week she puts fresh flowers on his grave.' He finished his brandy.

'She owns the house she lives in and also has a little finca out in the country. She was telling me that with her husband dead the land is no longer tilled even though it is very rich. The almond trees are so heavy in crop that she thinks there will be more sackfuls than ever before. And the algarroba beans are thicker than fleas on a dog. If she were married, her husband would have a rich property.'

'And a vinegary wife.'

'Don't you men ever learn ... ' She controlled her hasty temper. She ran the palm of her hand over her jet-black hair, then said in a much calmer voice: 'A man can't have everything.'

'With her, he'd lack peace.'

'If a man has rich fields to work in, heavy trees to harvest, and fat animals to slaughter, of what account is it if his wife has a tongue which at times is a little sharp?'

'Hers is razor-edged: all the time.'

Dolores drew a deep breath.

'What time's grub?'

She still managed to speak calmly. 'It may be a little late. Teresa has been visiting a friend in Inca and the bus will not have arrived back in the village yet.'

He looked at his watch. 'If she's going to be very long I'll have to grab a quick bite on my own.'

'What on earth do you mean?'

'I must leave here by nine-thirty.'

'To go where?'

'To watch the folk dancing in the square.'

She put her hands on her hips, her voice finally rose to strident tones, and her eyes sparkled with sharp anger. 'Since when have you been interested in folk dancing?' 'I'm sorry, but how was I to know you were laying on a special meal? And what's it matter if I'm not around?'

'You men!' she shouted. 'I try to help you and all you do is mock me. I even invite that ... that woman here although she has the tongue of a snake and no one's safe from her poison ... But you ... Too selfish ever to worry about the sacrifices I make. You do just as you want without reference to anyone else. So now I'm cooking a meal fit for the queen and it's going to be her who eats it whilst you ... ' She whirled round and stamped off into the kitchen, slamming the door shut behind herself.

*

Alvarez sat in his office and stared without interest at the paperwork on his desk. Was a man never too old to make a fool of himself? But her eyes were like Juana-Maria's had been, her character was as open and honest as Juana-Maria's had been ...

What was he? An unsuccessful detective, despised or at best forgotten by his superiors, living for the day he retired on a pension. A man who owned not as much as a tumble-down caseta or even a few hundred square metres of land. To look in a mirror was to be faced by middle-aged failure. Yet last night they had laughed and after the folk dancing she had insisted they dance together even though he had told her that he danced like an elephant with a wooden leg ... So was it just possible that when she looked at him she did not see him as he was, but as he might have been?

The phone rang.

'This is the Institute of Forensic Anatomy,' said the woman with the scratchy voice. 'The results of the final tests are now to hand in the case of Señorita Spiller. Traces of chloral hydrate were found in the contents of her stomach. Do you know what that is?'

'No, señorita.'

'It is a hypnotic which can be taken orally or intravenously. If taken orally, it may produce either severe drowsiness or full unconsciousness, depending on how much is taken. It has a bitter taste which is not easily concealed.'

Mickey Finn, he thought, wondering why the fool woman couldn't have said so at the beginning.

'It is impossible to estimate precisely the amount she ingested, but Professor Ramis is of the opinion that the deceased was probably never wholly unconscious although largely unaware of what she was doing.

'Finally, with reference to the samples you sent us very recently, one of these, labelled kitchen, contained a high proportion of alcohol.'

After replacing the receiver, he leaned back in the chair. So it had been murder. Doped, she had been guided out on to the balcony and pushed over to fall to her death, her reactions so dulled that she had not even screamed. Back in the flat, the scene had been set for accidental death, following a bout of drinking. Had Brenda not called at the apartment on Wednesday and then phoned the police with her suspicions, accidental death it would almost certainly have been.

Murder presupposed a motive. Who but Finnister had a motive for murdering a lonely woman, ignored or disliked by almost all the other foreigners? And yet Finnister ...

He telephoned Superior Chief Salas's office.

'Well?' snapped Salas, typically not bothering with any polite greeting.

Alvarez detailed the facts of the case as they now stood.

'Why haven't you arrested Finnister?'

'Señor, the man is ... Well, he's too weak to commit a murder.'

'It doesn't take much strength to push a half-conscious woman over a balcony.'

'I didn't really mean strength in that respect. I was referring to his character: he has no moral fibre.'

'What murderer has?'

It was so difficult to put into words exactly what he meant. A murderer had to have sufficient will-power to carry out his act, knowing what the result would be ...

Salas impatiently broke into his thoughts. 'His lighter was in the flat, and stubs of the cigarettes he smokes. Were his prints on any of the bottles?'

'I haven't had time to check yet.'

'What the devil do you mean, not had time?'

He listened to a short, but sharp, lecture on efficiency and gloomily agreed that he would check the bottles immediately. There was a further lecture on initiative, before Salas closed by saying that he wanted the case cleared up very, very smartly.

He slumped back in the chair. Who was he to say that desperation might not have supplied Finnister with the will power he normally lacked? Yet Finnister must surely know that the señorita never drank gin, so wouldn't he have left out a bottle of sherry to back up the probability of accident? But to accept this was to accept that the murderer had not known the señorita's habits very well. How, then, could he have had cause to murder her ... ?

The motives for murder were usually stereotyped and by far the most common were sex and money. It seemed unlikely that she could ever have given cause for a sexually based murder. Money? She had not been wealthy, yet she had promised Finnister she would find someone who would give her the two hundred thousand pesetas he so desperately needed. Whom had she known who had been wealthy?

*

'Who?' demanded Agnes.

'Inspector Alvarez, Cuerpo General de Policia, señora,' replied the maid.

Agnes heaved herself up from the chair and then leaned forward to pick up the balance sheets at which she had been working. She locked these in the small safe in the room that was her office.

She went down the short passage and into the larger of the two sitting-rooms. Large, airy, it contained magnificent French furniture, Persian carpets, French Post-Impressionist paintings, and a bow-fronted display cabinet of early Chelsea porcelain, all of which she had bought over the years at bargain prices: strangely, for so gross a person, she had a love and a flair for antiques.

She said curtly to Alvarez: 'I'm very busy, so I can't waste time. What is it?' She flopped down on to a tapestry-covered William and Mary chair.

'I am very sorry to trouble you, señora ... '

'Never mind all that: just tell me what you want?'

She had not asked him to sit. Standing, he said: 'I understand that you knew Señorita Spiller, who so unfortunately died on Tuesday?'

'She worked part-time for me as secretary.'

'Will you please tell me, did you agree to give or to lend to her two hundred thousand pesetas just before she died?'

'Of course not.'

'You are quite certain, señora?'

She contemptuously ignored the question.

He went on: 'The señorita had great need of that money to give to her fiancé.'

'I told her at the beginning that that man was marrying her for the very little money she had.'

'She did not give him the money before she died, but it seems she was quite certain she was to receive it. If it was not to come from you, can you suggest who might have been going to give it to her?'

'I cannot.'

'The person would have to be quite rich.'

'Not as I understand the meaning of the word "rich".'

'But for the ordinary person ... '

'I know nothing about the matter and there is absolutely no point in discussing it any further.'

He hesitated, then thanked her for her help. She nodded curtly and rang the bell for the maid because she was not going to have him walking to the front door unaccompanied: there were several quite valuable pieces of bric-a-brac in the hall and she knew that all the islanders were light-fingered.

*

Cosgrove dived into the pool and swam under water to the shallow end. When he surfaced and looked up, Gina was standing by the steps.

'I had to speak to you.' She was wearing a simple but well-cut cotton frock which moulded her body without being too obvious: she looked very beautiful.

He stood and climbed the steps out of the pool. The sun beat down on his bronzed, muscular body.

'I've been expecting you to come round to my place,' she said, nervously.

'Life has been rather hectic recently. How about a drink in the shade? I've had about enough sun for the moment ... Well, how's my favourite blonde getting on? Leading the usual frenetic life?'

'Blane, I ... '

He looked quizzically at her, but when she merely blinked rapidly and gulped he walked round the pool to the patio. She followed him, wishing that her tears weren't so near to falling.

It was not much cooler under the patio, but at least they were out of the direct glare of the sun. He asked her what she wanted and left to go inside and she stared out at the pool and the garden and wondered with fresh bitterness why the world was so generous to few and so mean to the many.

He returned, put the glasses on the table, and sat. 'Here's to us,' he said, as he raised his glass.

'That's not going to do much good.'

'How can you be miserable on so glorious a day as this?'

'You know damn well.'

'You're not still worrying about your little trouble?'

'Of course I bloody well am.'

He offered her a cigarette and flicked open the lighter.

'You've got everything. I've never had anything,' she said bitterly.

'For someone with nothing, you've managed to lead a pretty hectic life.'

That was true. There had been the parties, the wild drives ending in midnight swims, the champagne dances at the Parelona Hotel, the quick trips to Paris, Rome, Madrid ... 'Why shouldn't I have fun?' she demanded.

'No reason at all.'

She stared beseechingly at him. 'Blane, you've got to help me.' When he made no answer, she burst out: 'Damn it, you're the father.'

'I might be the father. But then so might any number of other men.'

She finally began to cry.

'You're turning it all into unnecessary melodrama: the days of the outstretched arm and the front doorstep are over. A quick trip to England and all your little troubles are over.'

'I've told you, I can't have an abortion.'

'I suppose you know that there's no future in martyrdom.'

'Won't you ... ' Somehow, despite his previous attitude, she had managed to persuade herself that if she appealed to him again he would either marry her or let her move into his house. But now looking at him through tear-blurred eyes she understood that she had been a naive fool.

'Five hundred pounds on top of medical fees and travel costs,' he said.

'Why won't you understand? I can't make myself do something I know is terribly wrong.'

'Excellent principles, but no sense of proportion.'

She stubbed out the cigarette with a force that split the paper.

'Look at things realistically, Gina. There's something about motherhood which douses a man's ardour. Have the kid and you'll find the invitations trailing right off.'

'Some men aren't the bastards that you are.'

'Some men are saints. But one has to travel a long way to find them.'

She stood.

'Rushing off in a huff won't solve anything, but it will lose you a lunch at the yacht club.'

She longed to go, to turn her back on the life she had known, but even while she longed she knew that she had lost the courage to break away from it before it deserted her. Slowly, with more tears rolling down her cheeks, she sat.

Chapter Fourteen

Alvarez, grunting from the effort, bent down. He inserted a thin bamboo into the last of the empty tonic bottles on the floor in the sitting-room of Miriam's flat, lifted it, and carried it over to the table on which were laid a camel's-hair brush, a bottle of print powder, and a dry saucer with some of the steel-grey powder poured into it. Continuing to hold the bamboo in his left hand, he painted powder over the bottle. One set of finger prints became visible: thumb and one finger up on the neck, the other three fingers running down the bottle in a rough arc. On the dressing-table in the main bedroom the silver-backed hairbrush had provided some excellent comparison prints and these now identified the prints on the bottle as being Miriam's.

He left the bottle on the table, next to the others, and crossed to a chair and slumped down on it. Miriam's prints were on three of the bottles, there were no other prints on any of them: normally he would have expected to find many prints because these bottles must have been handled by a number of people. Probably the murderer had wiped them clean before making certain that she handled them.

Assume Finnister could nerve himself to murder, did he have the kind of mind that would set the scene to be an accident yet would accept the possibility that the police might not be taken in and so would make certain that the prints on the empty bottles were just hers and not his? Yet if he were that clever, why hadn't he remembered that she did not drink gin? If Finnister had not murdered her, who else had had the motive ... ?

Who had been going to give or lend her the two hundred thousand pesetas? Or had the promise never existed and had she talked about it merely to try and push some backbone into Finnister ... ?

He sighed, looked at his watch. It was late Saturday afternoon and so nothing more could be done until Monday morning. Satisfied, he relaxed. Tonight, he thought with youthful excitement, he was taking Brenda to watch the battle between the Moors and the Christians.

Dressed in cream-coloured pyjamas – loose jackets and trousers which came to just below the knees – armed with swords, staves, and guns, the

Christians rallied. Two of their number, about to dive into the nearest bar, were grabbed just before they disappeared and unceremoniously thrust to the forefront. Calling on God, the Christians advanced.

The Moors, faces, necks, and chests blackened, in baggy clothes of vivid hues, their scimitars flashing, cried to Allah to support them in their hour of need as they stubbornly defended.

The narrow street rang to the din of battle and the cries of the wounded went unheeded as the two forces became locked in mortal combat.

'All right, move on a bit,' shouted the municipal policeman.

The Moors retreated, the Christians advanced.

Brenda, having to shout to make herself heard, asked: 'Doesn't anyone ever get hurt?'

'Only a few broken limbs,' answered Alvarez carelessly.

The last three Moors carried between them a vast old muzzle loader, two metres long, its barrel bound with wire, its wooden butt badly worm-eaten. They set this down on the road, facing the Christians, who prudently came to an abrupt halt. One of the Moors poured powder into the muzzle.

'My God, surely they're not actually going to fire that thing, are they?' she asked.

'Why not?'

'It can't be safe: it'll explode.'

'It never has yet,' he reassured her.

The third Moor primed the gun and then applied a slow-burning match. There was an explosion which rocked the street and produced a rolling cloud of sulphurous smoke. Brenda gave a strangled scream and grabbed hold of Alvarez's arm. 'I can't stand bangs,' she exclaimed.

Two of the Christians declared themselves well and truly shot and hurried back to the bar from which they had been withheld earlier while those of stouter heart, or not quite so thirsty, shouted their war-cry and prepared to advance. The three Moors picked up the gun and retreated. The tide of battle flowed away from them and when the next explosion shattered the air it did no more than make her start.

'They're slowly making their way to the football ground,' he explained, 'where there's the last and decisive battle and the two heroes, Benito and Felix, capture the gun and turn it on the Moors to kill dozens of them before they get killed themselves. They saved the village.'

'But the Christians have been having the best of the battle from the beginning.'

He grinned. 'Sometimes, history changes a little to make the facts more acceptable. The Moors arrived in the middle of the night – which is why the Christians are wearing night-clothes – and created such panic that they very nearly took the village with the villagers running in all directions. Luckily, Benito and Felix, a couple of ne'er-do-wells who much earlier had pinched a hogshead of wine from some soldiers and drunk themselves silly, came to and dragged themselves out of the pig-sty in which they'd collapsed and surprised the Moors with the gun. They mistook the Moors for the soldiers who were looking for the wine and as there was no chance of breaking free they attacked them and somehow managed to kill them. They reckoned the gun must be worth a peseta or two and began to carry it away with them when they came on the main body of the Moors. This sobered them up sufficiently to suddenly realize what was really happening, and since there wasn't anything else they could do they fired the gun. The villagers saw the Moors being mown down and thought reinforcements had arrived and so they rallied and between them beat the Moors back.'

'What happened to Benito and Felix?'

'Like all true heroes, they were found dead, surrounded by all the Moors they'd slain.'

'You're making the story up as you go along.'

'It's fact. Why else should every bar in the village stay open for three days and nights if not to honour the two drunkards? ... Shall we go to the football pitch and watch the last battle?'

'Do they fire the gun there?'

'Several times.'

'Then I'd rather be as far away as possible and not risk adding to its list of victims.'

He looked at his watch. 'Tonight, the restaurants serve the same meal as the villagers ate after their thanksgiving service. I've booked a table even though I couldn't ask you until now. You will come with me, won't you?'

'I really ought to get back to the port to see that everyone's happy ... But, yes, I will and for once to hell with the paying customers!'

'Wonderful!' he exclaimed, his face lighting up.

'What will we be eating? Chick peas and dry bread?'

'Grilled fish, sucking pig, and cream cake ... I think that perhaps here also history has been altered just a little.'

*

On Monday morning, Cosgrove phoned Agnes. 'Blane here. I thought you'd be glad to know that everything's been wrapped up.'

'Have you got the deeds?'

'Not yet, but there's no problem: they're all in order.'

'The moment you have them, send them to my solicitor.'

He chuckled. 'I wonder if you ever trust anyone?'

She said an abrupt goodbye and cut the connection.

He replaced the receiver, crossed to the front door and opened this to step out on to the porch. He thought, as he stared at the flower-beds which flanked the drive and were ablaze with colour, how vulnerable a really suspicious person was.

At a quarter to twelve, Alvarez replaced the phone in his office and leaned back in the chair. The last of the banks on the island had just confirmed that Señorita Spiller had not banked with them. So her only account had been with the Caja de Ahorros y Monte de Piedad de Las Baleares in the Port.

If she had not had two hundred thousand pesetas herself, and there was no one living locally who would have given or lent it to her, had she hoped to obtain it in England? Yet if such person lived in England, could he or she be involved in the señorita's murder on this island? Or did the large sum of money not hold the significance he now placed on it ... ?

He must ask England to check on her past life.

*

Alvarez knocked on the door of Brenda's flat and after a while she opened the door. 'Sorry about the delay, but I was just out of the shower when the bell rang.'

'And I am sorry to disturb you, but I have to speak to you.'

She smiled. 'You make it sound a matter of great solemnity. Come on in.'

He entered and closed the door. 'You'll have a drink, won't you?' she asked. He replied that he'd love one.

She led the way into the sitting-room, asked him what he'd like, and then prepared the drinks. He watched her. She had the economy of movement that all naturally graceful people possessed. She didn't look her age of 41. True there were lines about her eyes and mouth, but her curly brown hair was untouched by grey and in her dark brown eyes there was the sparkle of life which meant a person was young however many the years ...

'Here you are. And it's my turn to propose the toast. Happiness!'

They clinked glasses and then she went over to the settee and sat. 'What's brought you here?'

'As you know, I have been making enquiries into the death of Señorita Spiller. I can now say for certain that it was not an accident, she was murdered.'

'It's horrible to think that someone could deliberately have killed her ... Do you know why?'

'That is what I am trying to find out now, but it is very difficult because she was such a solitary person ... I need to learn where she was going to obtain the money she wished to give to Señor Finnister. It seems it cannot have been coming from anyone here so perhaps she knew someone rich in England. I will ask the English police to find out. Do you know where she used to live?'

'Beyond the fact that it was in Brighton, no. And I wouldn't know that if once, when she was more than usually depressed, she hadn't told me how much she longed to return to Brighton, but couldn't.'

'Did she say for certain, couldn't?'

'That's right.'

'Do you know why this was so?'

'No.' She drank, then held her glass on her lap. 'You were so right when you said she was a solitary woman: she was intensely secretive and I learned virtually nothing about her past – not that I ever tried to.'

'I believe that all her money came from a pension?'

'It was paid by the firm for whom she had worked.'

He said thoughtfully: 'Was she, perhaps, not a little young for a pension?'

'Now you mention it, I suppose she was. She never told me her age – a deadly secret – but I suppose she was in her early fifties and most women don't usually retire until they're sixty if they're in full-time jobs. She certainly can't have been sixty.'

'She was fifty-three: I have checked her residencia ... Perhaps she retired because of ill-health?'

'She always seemed as fit as a fiddle, probably because she was so thin and stringy.' She smiled. 'It's people of my girth who run into trouble.'

'We have a saying, "The best aubergines grow on the thickest plants".'

'Very comforting if you're an aubergine, otherwise a little two-edged.'

'I'm afraid a farmer always measures beauty by his crops.'

He judged from her changed expression that suddenly she was back with those acres of land and woods she had so loved. 'I am very sorry,' he said quietly.

She started. 'Sorry about what?'

'Have I not reminded you of your land and home?'

She frowned. 'How did you know?'

'The look on your face.'

'Was it that much of a give-away? ... On a late summer evening when all the shadows were stretching out there used to be a special sheen to all the different shades of green, as if they'd been touched with dew ... ' She shrugged her shoulders and spoke far more briskly. 'But it's no good looking back: that only provokes a crick in the neck. How's your glass?'

He held it up to show it was still full.

'Didn't I mix it properly?'

He smiled. How long was it since he'd last been content to hold a glass in his hand and not drink from it?

*

Superior Chief Salas said over the phone: 'You've still not arrested Finnister?'

'No, señor,' replied Alvarez. 'As I have tried to explain, I find it very difficult to accept that he murdered the señorita.'

'Yet you've discovered no one else with a motive.'

'That is true, which is why I am asking that my enquiry be sent to the police in Brighton. It's possible we'll learn something when we know more bout the señorita's past life.'

'Have you questioned Finnister again?'

'Yes, señor. His story doesn't change.'

'Can't you break his alibi?'

'He has none, therefore I cannot break it.'

'Didn't anyone see him near the apartment block at the time of her death?'

'No, no one.'

'I suppose you have actually bothered to make such enquiries?'

'Indeed, señor.'

'Regrettably, there is no "indeed" about it,' snapped Salas, before ringing off.

*

The reply to his enquiries reached Alvarez on the Wednesday, at four-fifteen in the afternoon.

Miriam Anne Spiller, aged fifty-three. Previous address, in UK, 26 Winslow Avenue, Brighton, Sussex. Resided at that address, a council house, for thirty-one years, originally with her parents, then when her father died with her mother, lastly after her mother's death nearly four years ago, on her own. No known living relatives. Few acquaintances and impossible to discover anyone who had been in contact with her within past three years.

Prior to leaving Brighton she had worked for Beach and Thrush, a firm concerned with the sale of villas and apartments in Spain. Firm suspected of fraud and investigated. Death of one partner and disappearance of other with all the capital resulted in bankruptcy of firm. Staff dismissed. Miriam Spiller continued to live in Brighton at same address for short time, after which left for unknown destination. No further information available.

Chapter Fifteen

Alvarez stared at the slash of brilliant sunshine which burst through the window of his office to highlight a host of dancing specks. A firm which went bankrupt didn't pay pensions and Miriam had not been old enough to qualify for the state pension – yet here, in Mallorca, she had claimed to be living on a pension and about forty-two thousand pesetas had been paid into her bank each month. When she had needed two hundred thousand pesetas she had known a 'friend' who would give, or lend, the money to her – yet she had no rich friends in England and the only rich person she had appeared to know on the island had contemptuously denied the possibility of having promised to provide the money.

She had worked for a firm which had gone bankrupt after enquiries concerning the possibility of fraud and one partner had died and the other had disappeared with a large sum of money. Had she known about the fraud and either been party to it or else refrained from reporting it in return for a 'pension'? And had her further demand for two hundred thousand pesetas been mistakenly seen as the beginning of a more onerous blackmail so that the blackmailer had killed her?

Was her character such that she would have connived at fraud? On the face of things, no. She was the kind of woman to be found in many offices, old beyond her years, dried up, gaining some sort of satisfaction from running an office with a loyalty beyond doubt ...

Yet who was to say what dreams, long dreamed, lay behind the appearance? Even the ugliest of women could long to be married ... But any man invited to Miriam's house would have met her mother – widowed, perhaps grown querulous – and he would have understood that mother would come too. So he would have moved on. As the years passed, so the chance of marriage faded: as it faded, so the desire for it became more intense. So intense, in fact, that when a man proposed not marriage, but a new, exciting life, in exchange for help in perpetrating a fraud or for her silence over her discovery of the fraud, she had suddenly thrown aside the character the world had always seen and listened to those nearly forgotten dreams ...

At first, the new life in Puerto Llueso had waved no magic wand and she had been as lonely and as thwarted as she had been back in Brighton: perhaps even lonelier, even more thwarted, because here it was always spring for love. But then she had met Frank Finnister. Not a whole man, true, but a man who had proposed. First the engagement ring. But then before the wedding ring ... He had desperately needed a large sum of money to prevent his being deported from Spain. She had believed she dare not return to England ...

Alvarez began to drum on the desk with his fingers. He must ask England for full details of the fraud and for a description of the missing partner ... He stood up, crossed to the window, and looked down at the street, cut in two by shadow. If he were right, a woman had met her death because she had so desperately wanted to get married: what more tragic trigger for murder could there be than that?

*

The manager of the Caja de Ahorros y Monte de Piedad de Las Baleares was young, smart, and efficient: there was a strong hint of Arab in his features. 'Yes, of course I remember you asking me about the señorita's account – something like a week ago. And then there was a further request for information from head office. You're still having trouble with the case, then?'

'Still having trouble,' agreed Alvarez heavily.

'So what can I do for you this time?'

'You told me she paid in around forty-two thousand pesetas every month – I need to know where that money came from.'

'That's going to be a job unless one of the blokes can remember. Hang on and I'll find out for you.' The manager stood, pushed his chair back, and left the room.

On the wall were three posters, hanging loose, one of which advertised the fact that the bank would grant mortgages and the present rate of interest was 12½ % ... Ten years ago, Alvarez thought, a million pesetas would have bought a house with land: today, it would buy nothing ...

The manager returned. 'You're in luck. It seems the señorita always made a point of dealing with Bernardo: must be his pale blue eyes. He says she always paid in cash, in pesetas.'

Alvarez plucked at his lower lip, not aware that he was doing this. Assume the money she received was being paid to her to keep quiet, then the fact that the payment was regular and in pesetas must argue the probability that the payer lived on the island.

He stood. 'Thanks a lot.'

'Glad to help, any time.'

As he turned, he saw the poster again. 'By the way ... What are the chances of getting a mortgage these days?'

The manager audibly drew in his breath to show a professional reluctance to commit himself. 'Things have become very tough, you know, especially with this latest oil crisis. We've always had to submit applications to head office with our assessment of the applicant's credit-worthiness, but in the past it's been automatic for the mortgage to be granted if we recommend it – now, it's far from automatic.'

'But if you know the bloke well?'

'Depends who and what. Just occasionally, we can still twist head office's arm a little.' He studied Alvarez with open interest. 'Are you asking for yourself?'

'It's just I'm kind of curious,' he replied hastily.

'If you do apply, I'd say you'd have no trouble. For some reason, policemen are viewed as a good risk!'

'How much does one get now?'

'Forty per cent of our valuation on the house and land.'

'Is that all?'

'That's all, Enrique. We used to be able to offer a higher percentage, but not now.'

'But if a reasonable flat costs at least three million, one has to find ... ' He stopped as he began to work out the figures. 'The buyer has to be able to put down a deposit of one million eight hundred thousand.'

'What are the repayments?'

'Maximum of twelve years – but for the first two years it need be only the interest repaid: that's to give the poor bloke a breathing space before he has to cough up one tenth of the capital as well! But if you're seriously trying to cost the whole thing out, don't forget the fees, as so many people do. Take a three million peseta flat. For tax purposes, that's declared at around five hundred thousand. But the government knows it's a gross under-valuation, so they bump up the rate of the taxes ... All in all, solicitor's, bank's, and notario's fees added to the taxes means you're talking about a hundred thousand expenses, give or take a few thousand.'

That was on top of the cost of the house and of furnishing it! Sweet Mary, now a man had to be rich even to buy a poor man's house.

'Don't look so gloomy. With inflation booming, a house'll be the best investment you ever make.'

But where did a mere inspector find the deposit of one million eight hundred thousand? And how out of his salary – which did not reflect the booming rate of inflation – did he find the interest and, two years later, the capital repayments as well ... ?

'I'll tell you the perfect solution, Enrique. Marry a rich foreigner.'

'What?' he snapped.

'Hang on, I was only joking.' The manager hastened to correct what had obviously been a faux pas.

Alvarez slowly crossed to the door.

'Any time you want seriously to talk about a mortgage, come along and I'll do what I can for you.'

He left the bank, walked to the nearest café, ordered a brandy and a coffee, and sat. A foreigner had swindled his parents out of the land which had been worth a hundred times what he had paid them for it. A foreigner in a car had pinned Juana-Maria against a wall, crushing her to death. Foreigners had pushed the price of houses sky-high, so that a man could not afford to buy one should he marry a ... a foreigner. God had created all men fools, turning their hatreds into their desires ...

He left the café, ignoring a cheery greeting from a man who had just entered, walked down to the front and stared at the scene. Luxury yachts, luxury restaurants, luxury cars, people corrupted by luxury ... Oh to be given the chance to be corrupted!

He continued along the front, passing the western arm of the harbour, to Finnister's flat. He climbed the creaking stairs.

Finnister's shrill greeting was in character. 'Why do you keep on persecuting me? I've told you, I never went near her flat. Why won't you believe me? I didn't know she'd left me anything in her will and even if I had, I'd never have killed her for it. I couldn't kill anyone. For God's sake, why can't you see that?'

'I think I can, señor. But others cannot. Superior Chief Salas does not understand why I have not arrested you days ago for the murder of the señorita.'

'What?' he screamed.

'I am afraid he is rather an impatient man.'

'I never went near her flat on Tuesday. I was working ... '

'Señor, let me assure you that there is no need to tell me everything again.'

Finnister ran his fingers through his hair in a wild gesture of total despair. 'I can't work with all this going on. Why can't anyone understand what it's like for an artist? I must have peace of mind. Could Proust have completed À La Recherche Du Temps Perdu if ten times a day he had been hounded by the minions of the law?' Alvarez waited.

Finnister sat down on a wooden chair whose rush seat was badly frayed. 'A man can only stand so much.'

'I must ask you some more questions ... '

'Stop tormenting me!'

'But if I do not ask you more questions, señor, I can never be certain who murdered the señorita. Then I shall have to arrest you on the orders of my superior chief and you will be sent to jail.'

His voice became shriller. 'They use the garotte. You're put in a chair with your hands and legs lashed down and a thin cord is looped round your neck and then it's tightened ... '

'No one has been garotted in Spain for several years now and in any case I understand that it is quite quick.'

'Is that supposed to reassure me?'

'It is surely better than learning that it is very slow?'

He jumped to his feet. 'I can't stay on this island another day ... '

'Señor, for the moment you must stay and in order to help persuade you that this is so, I must have your passport before I leave here.'

He collapsed back on to the chair.

'If you are truly innocent, tell me everything you know about the señorita so that I may discover what really happened.'

'I've told you, over and over again, but you won't listen ... '

'Señor, you have never answered this before. Did the señorita meet a man somewhere on this island at the beginning of each month?'

'Of course she didn't.'

'But can you be so certain, if you work in this flat each day?'

'She would have told me all about it. When we became engaged, we promised each other there would be no secrets between us.'

'Then you had informed the señorita about your friend who lives in Calle Pescadores?'

'I ... She was different,' he said, with offended dignity.

103

'Then might not the señorita also have had some meetings which were different?'

'You're not trying to suggest she had a lover?'

'Señor, I think that is most unlikely. But might she not have had another motive for hiding such meetings from you?'

'She didn't know anyone. People were either too snooty to talk to her or she got all uptight and didn't want to have anything to do with them.'

'Did she travel to somewhere on this island at the beginning of each month?'

'She never went anywhere.'

'But she must surely have gone somewhere, some time?'

'Only to the library in Playa Nueva.'

'Did you go with her?'

'No. It was a hopeless library. They didn't have a single one of my books.'

'How often did she visit there?'

'I don't know. Maybe every fortnight, when she ran out of the tripe she would insist on reading.'

'Did she drive there?'

'She took the bus. She hadn't a car and anyway she'd never learned to drive.'

'Can you remember any other journeys she made regularly?'

'There weren't any.'

'It might help you a great deal if you could think of more.'

'There weren't any. Shall I say it again. There weren't any. There weren't any.'

'Then I need disturb you no longer.' He paused. 'But just before I leave, perhaps I may have your passport?'

Finnister looked as if he were going to cry.

Chapter Sixteen

Agnes – a redhead, with Southern Belle waves and curls – left her car and crossed to the steps leading up to the porch of Cosgrove's house. She climbed them, her face set in lines of bitter anger which, however, were not immediately apparent because they tended to get lost in the folds of flesh. She rang the bell and Marta opened the door. 'Good morning, señora ... '

Agnes swept past her. 'Where the hell are you?' she shouted. Then, through the windows of the sitting-room, she saw him as he sunbathed, face downwards, by the side of the pool.

'I will tell ... ' began Marta.

'I will tell him,' she snapped. She crossed to the right-hand french door out on to the patio and pulled it open so energetically that it crashed back against a window. Cosgrove looked up in time to see her march out.

'This is a very unexpected pleasure.' He rolled over and came to his feet.

'I warned you right from the beginning.'

'Warned me?' He looked ironically surprised. 'Perhaps we ought to go and sit down in the patio. And unless you really do want to include my neighbours in the conversation, it'll pay to speak a little more quietly.'

She stared at him, noticing his smooth, confident smile. Her own lips lay in a hard, straight line.

He led the way into the shade of the patio and pulled out a chair for her. 'Can I get you something to drink?'

'This isn't a social call.'

He laughed. 'There's one thing for certain, you always make your feelings abundantly clear.'

She sat and the metal frame of the chair squeaked briefly as her weight came on it. 'My solicitor phoned me earlier on.'

'Señor Covas? To tell the truth, I was quite impressed by him. He struck me as completely straightforward.'

'He's read through the deeds.'

'Then I'm even more impressed. Honest and on the ball!'

'Who is Renato Goñi?'

'The person from whom we bought the land. That surely was quite clear?'

'Stop trying to treat me like a bloody fool,' she shouted. He looked at her enquiringly.

She forced herself to calm down. She leaned forward and he noticed that her breath was stale. 'Until a few months ago, that land was owned by a man called Palasi, who'd inherited it from his father.'

'Was that his name? I don't remember.'

'He sold it for two million pesetas. Yet you told me you were buying the land from the man whose family had owned it for years.'

'I certainly never said that.'

'Maybe not in so many words, but that's exactly what you implied. It's no good trying to deny it.'

'I'm afraid I have to. I implied nothing.'

'Covas tried to contact Goñi in order to clear up some point, or other. He doesn't live in Santa Veronica any more and no one knows where he's gone to.'

'Is there something wrong with the deeds?'

'No, not wrong enough to matter. But Covas ... '

'Then surely it doesn't matter what's happened to Goñi?'

'It matters a hell of a lot. It's obvious that you've been using him as a front.' She slammed her hand down on the glass topped table. 'You bought the land in Goñi's name for two million and then told me we'd have to pay thirty million to buy it and bribe the council, because the owner had put the price up knowing what the place would be worth with development permission.' She hit the table a second time. 'A friend of mine's been checking up. There's not the slightest chance that permission to develop will ever be given: the mayor's rabidly communistic.' Her voice rose yet again. 'You've swindled me out of fifteen million pesetas.'

'Is that Covas's opinion?'

She snorted. 'D'you think any lawyer ever has the courage to call a spade a spade? But I have. I know I'm dealing with a swindler.'

'You're using pretty strong language.'

'Swindler,' she shouted.

'Prove it,' he said calmly.

'You tricked me from the beginning.'

'On the contrary, I did all I could to discourage you from becoming my partner: in fact, you even had to blackmail me into accepting you. Covas will confirm at least the important part of what I've just said ... Don't you remember when we were in his office that I put all the risks to you, to give you a last chance of withdrawing? You refused to be put off.'

'I didn't understand that you'd already swindled me ... You knew we would never get planning permission: you've never even tried to obtain it. The whole story was made up to get my fifteen million. But I'm telling you, you're not going to get away with it. I'll expose you in the courts.'

'I'm sure you put your incredible suspicions to Covas. What did he make of them?'

She hesitated.

'I imagine that, remembering how carefully and fully I put things to you in his presence, he said something to the effect that it would be very difficult to justify and prove your suspicions. Perhaps he added that only if Goñi could be traced and if it could be proved beyond any shadow of a doubt he was acting as my front man and that the intention of the sale of the land to our partnership was fraudulent in nature and not merely a smart piece of business, could you possibly have any sort of action against me? And perhaps he added that in his opinion none of this was possible?'

Her eyes prickled with tears of bitter frustration. 'Agnes, I think you're overwrought, perhaps because you're not used to having a largish sum of money out at risk. So suppose we forget all the unpleasant things you've been saying ... '

'I'll forget nothing,' she said viciously.

'Surely it would be rather more dignified?'

'Who do you think you are to talk about dignity? A bloody little jumped-up clerk from outer Ealing?' She noticed his changed expression, and, like any skilled fighter exploiting an opponent's weakness, she attacked with redoubled vigour. 'You surely didn't really believe that any of us were fooled? You may have a little money and a silver tongue, but it stands out a mile that you've even less background than a peasant. When I've finished telling people how you've swindled me, there won't be a decent home on the island will receive you.'

He struggled to keep his tone light, but was aware that it was betraying his sudden wild anger. 'You're actually going to admit that you, so tough and smart that no one on God's earth can outsmart you, have been taken for fifteen million pesetas? Don't you realize that there isn't a soul in Mallorca who hasn't been longing for you to come a cropper? You'll become the laughing stock of the island.'

Trembling, she stood. 'You'll pay for this.'

'At least my payment will be deferred: yours has been in advance.'

She turned and ran through the sitting-room and hall to the front door which she slammed open. Back on the patio, he stared out at the pool. The words, 'Bloody little jumped up clerk from outer Ealing' kept repeating themselves in his mind.

*

The library, once a small shop, was on the outskirts of Puerto Playa Nueva and a few hundred metres to the west of it began the ribbon development which in just over ten years had changed a beautiful, curving, sandy bay, ringed by pine trees, into a concrete jungle. The library stocked mainly English books, but there was a small and growing selection of French and German ones.

Alvarez spoke to the woman – middle-aged, dressed in a flower-print cotton frock, as patently English as he was Mallorquin – who sat at a small desk.

'Oh, dear! A policeman! Have I done something wrong?'

'Señorita, do not disturb yourself. I am here just to ask questions concerning Señorita Spiller.'

'Poor Miriam.' She lowered her voice. 'It was a terrible, terrible shock: I can't tell you how dreadful I felt. I used to keep the latest Barbara Cartland and Denise Robbins for her ... '

Alvarez listened patiently until she paused and then he said: 'What I want to know is if Señorita Spiller regularly met someone here?'

'You're ... you're not suggesting ... ' Her eyes widened.

'I am suggesting nothing.'

'Oh!' She fiddled with a couple of filing cards. 'She never met anyone here – not regularly.'

'You can be certain of that?'

'Indeed, yes. In this kind of a job one naturally notices that sort of thing. I mean, one can't help it.'

'Please tell me what happened usually when she came here?'

'Well, she always arrived at roughly the same time because of course she came in the bus from Puerto Llueso. I'd show her any books I'd specially kept for her and we'd have a chat. She loved a good chat: rather lonely, you know. Then usually she'd go along to the café just up the road and have a coffee while she waited for the bus back. I've a friend who takes over now and then to give me a break and so sometimes I'd go and have coffee with Miriam. As I said, she loved a chat.'

'And did she meet someone at the café?'

'I can't say, since I only went there now and then, but when I did go Miriam was completely on her own. Who ... who do you think she might have been meeting?'

'I do not know. I wish I did.'

'I'm very sorry I can't help you.'

'It is kind of you to have tried,' he said formally. 'Goodbye, señorita.' He walked over to the open doorway.

'I say ... '

He turned back.

'I don't suppose ... Well, I've just remembered something, but I don't suppose it's really of any interest to you.'

'It may be of great interest, so please tell me.'

'Well, there was this one day when I didn't think I'd be able to get away, although I wanted to, and anyway Miriam had said she'd some shopping to do and so she left on her own. And then my friend turned up and offered to look after the library for half an hour, or so, and I went along to the chemist at the end of the road to buy some aspirins ... I've been getting a lot of headaches recently and it's not my eyes because I had them tested ... And when I looked in the café Miriam wasn't there, but after leaving the chemist I did see her, getting into a car.'

'Do you know whose car it was?'

'I've no idea. It was pointing the other way and I never saw who the driver was.'

'But there was a driver in it?'

'There must have been, mustn't there, because she couldn't drive.'

'Yes, of course. I was forgetting,' he said blandly. 'Can you say what make of car it was?'

'I'm afraid I don't know one from another.'

'And I suppose you've no idea of the registration number?'

She shook her head.

He shrugged his shoulders, a wry smile on his lips. 'Perhaps the policeman could tell you,' she said eagerly.

'Policeman?'

'The car was parked where it shouldn't have been and that horrid policeman who's always giving people parking tickets was by it and writing. I'll bet it hadn't been parked there for any time at all.'

'How long ago was this?'

'I suppose it must be about a couple of months.'

'And at what time of the month?'

'I don't really know, but she usually came here at the beginning and the middle of each month.'

He thanked her again.

Back in his office, which was hotter and stuffier than ever, Alvarez dialled the municipal police in Puerto Playa Nueva. 'I need a bit of help,' he told the man on the other end of the line.

'We're up to our eye-balls in work,' was the immediate reply.

'I'm told you've one particular bloke who's always hitting cars for bad parking – he could help me a lot. I need a list of all the cars and their owners who he's booked along the front road over the past four months.'

'You don't know what you're asking! He books scores of cars a day, especially when the municipal funds are low. What you're asking is virtually impossible.'

'Sorry, but it has to be done.'

'That's easy enough to say! But we have to work all day long without this sort of bloody nonsense turning up. We're not like you, sitting on your backside all day long, boozing.'

'And to think I never knew,' said Alvarez sarcastically, before ringing off.

He relaxed. After a while, he thought about the bottle of brandy in the bottom right-hand drawer of the desk. He brought it out and poured himself a drink.

Chapter Seventeen

Finnister looked up and down Calle Pescadores: several children were playing a jumping game with a very large loop of elastic, a couple of tourists, brick-red in colour from sunburn, were walking down the far pavement, and a cart, loaded with cut wood, whose driver was three parts asleep and leaving the mule to find its own way, was clopping along in the direction of the urbanizaciòn. He turned and stared at the door of No. 7, with its peeling paint, and then hastily knocked before he lost what little courage he still possessed.

Carol opened the door. She stared at him, her expression first one of surprise and then of growing fear. 'What are you doing here?' she demanded in a low voice.

'You never came this morning.'

'But I couldn't. Ted didn't go out boozing because he's no money left. You know I'd've come if I could. For God's sake, love, go away before there's trouble.'

'I've got to see you.'

'I can't, not with Ted here ... ' She was interrupted by a shout from the back room. 'Where are you?'

'For God's sake, clear off, love, before he sees you. He's in one of his real mean moods because he hasn't had any booze.'

'But I've just got to talk to you.'

She was almost crying from fear. 'Don't be so bleeding barmy. You know you can't talk here. If he was to find you ... '

There was a crashing sound from inside. 'What are you doing, you bitch? Who is it?'

'Please go,' she pleaded, with desperate urgency.

An inner door banged open. 'Come back in half an hour.' She slammed the outside door shut.

Through the door he heard her saying that their caller had been one of the neighbours, asking if she'd any plastic bags to spare. Ted shouted that she was lying and she'd been talking about him. Stumbling, because in his panic he tripped over his own feet, Finnister hurried away. Ted had the strength of an ox ...

For thirty minutes he walked the roads, only half-aware of where he was, his mind a playground of fears, then he returned to Calle Pescadores. The children were still playing their game with elastic and they giggled when they saw him.

He knocked on the door of No. 7 with trembling hand. Suppose she hadn't been able to calm Ted's suspicions so that right now he was waiting on the other side of the door ... ?

Carol opened the door.

'Is it all right?' he demanded breathlessly.

She nodded: her face was strained and white, her hair in a tangle, her dress crumpled at the collar.

He stepped inside and she shut the door. 'You oughtn't to have come here,' she said in a very low voice.

'The detective has been to my place again. He says his superior wants him to arrest me for Miriam's murder.'

'Oh, God, no!'

There was a blurred shout from the room beyond. 'What's up?'

He spoke wildly. 'You said it was all right to come in.'

'But I thought he was boozed silly.'

'Where are you, you bitch?' shouted Ted. They heard heavy footsteps and then he began to fiddle with the door knob.

'He'll kill me,' moaned Finnister. He ran to the front door and struggled to open it, but with the perversity of all inanimate objects in emergencies, the handle refused to turn. He could feel the avenging hands crashing down on him ...

She went into the inner room, slamming the door shut behind herself. There was more shouting, the sound of a blow, and a short scream. Finnister redoubled his efforts with the front-door handle, completely unaware that he was trying to turn it in the wrong direction. He heard the inner door open and almost fainted as the sweat stood out all over his body.

'He's out this time,' she said dully.

It was a while before her words penetrated his panic-soaked mind. 'Out?' he croaked.

'Pig-drunk unconscious.'

He let go of the handle, but did not move away from the door in case she was wrong for a second time.

'I made him finish the bottle I gave him.' She reached up and touched her cheek, where a bruise was just beginning to show. She desperately needed Finnister to comfort her and love the hurt away. She held out her arms to him.

'You know what they do in this country to murderers, don't you?' he said.

She slowly lowered her arms.

'They sit you in a chair and strap your arms and legs down and then they put a loop of cord round your neck and tighten it with a lever. They slowly choke you to death.'

'Oh, Frank,' she whimpered.

'You're trying to gulp down air and you can't and there's fire in your lungs and the agony grows until it tears your body apart ... '

She came forward, put her arms round him, and pressed his head against her breasts. The bruise on her cheek was now aching badly.

'I keep telling him I didn't kill her, but he won't listen. What am I to do?' he wailed.

'It'll be all right,' she whispered comfortingly.

*

An area of low pressure remained stationary over the north Sahara. By Friday, even the usual daytime breeze had been burned out of existence and the air was lifeless.

Shirt undone down the front, fan directed at his chest, Alvarez sat in his office and thought about the letter and the report from the Sussex police which had been brought from England by a member of the cabin staff of one of the planes, who had posted it in Palma, thus bypassing the three to four weeks minimum it took a letter to reach the island in the summer.

The details of the case were in parts complicated, although the theme was simple – fraud directed at people who were mostly retired and who had dreamed of owning a house in the sun.

The English company, Beach and Thrush, had advertised extensively and issued glossy, eye-catching brochures aimed at the newly retired. Near Marbella ('The Place where the Lovely People Live and Play') was a new urbanizaciòn in the course of construction whose motto was 'The best quality for the least money'. Every house, bungalow, or apartment was architecturally designed and offered a panoramic view of the sea while set amid gardens of unsurpassable beauty. Living there, retirement was something eagerly to be looked forward to, not feared: there, there was no such thing as old age, only ever-ripening middle-age ...

There had been viewing flights. Thirty-three pounds for the weekend, Saturday morning to Sunday night, and the money refunded if a unit was purchased. Hospitality in Spain had been lavish, with cheap sparkling white wine, masquerading as champagne, virtually on tap ... Nothing like a boozy weekend to persuade a couple that they'd better hurry and sign up for a slice of Shangri-La.

Incredibly, people had signed contracts without seeking legal advice, even without demanding a translation of the Spanish – the same people who in England would not have dreamed of buying the smallest property without consulting a solicitor. It seemed as if the concentration of sun, sea, and alcohol, had addled their wits ...

As time passed, some buyers regained sufficient sanity to become a trifle worried – where were the deeds to their properties? The representatives of Beach and Thrush were quick to point out that if the English law of property was complicated, the Spanish law of property was a mind-boggling jungle of incredibilities. So was it to be wondered at that the deeds were not as quickly forthcoming as they would have been in the UK? A pound sterling still bought four litres of red wine, so enjoy the sun and forget such mundane problems as missing deeds ...

In fact, the deeds were with various Spanish banks, placed with them as securities against loans made. Beach and Thrush thus made one profit on the building and selling of the properties (and as owners discovered, the urbanizaciòn's motto should have read 'The least quality for the most money'), a second profit on the mortgaging of it, and in several cases a third profit through their letting service for owners – they 'forgot' to account for rent received yet always remembered to account for repairs 'carried out'.

Inevitably, one or two owners finally became belligerently suspicious and they went to the police. The company was registered in England so although the properties in question were in Spain, the English police began investigating the company.

It took the police five and a half months to uncover sufficient evidence to be certain they were dealing with fraud and so could halt further trading and in this time the company took another sixty-two deposits on property 'which was in the course of building'. Sixty-two people lost their money, while another two hundred and eighty-seven discovered that in law they owned only a minority share in the houses they had bought and that to regain full ownership they would have to repay the mortgages. Almost all these unlucky owners had sold their homes in England in order to find the capital with which to buy in Spain and thus they either had no further capital available or else needed that capital to provide them with sufficient income to be able to live abroad. Over half the owners lost their homes and in only a handful of cases was there a meaningful sum of money left over after the banks were satisfied. Three men died within two months of the crash and although their death certificates listed coronary thromboses as the causes of death, it would have been almost as correct to have listed dreams in the sun ...

There had been two partners in Beach and Thrush: Colin Bonder and Anthony Moorhouse.

Naturally, police enquiries had centred on these two men, but the investigation, even after the police were certain there had been fraud, was a long and arduous one. And during the course of this investigation, the police met a large number of ordinary, nice people who had worked all their lives and had then been swindled and left shocked and financially shattered at a time when they had rightly expected to know quiet security. It was thus with a sense of angry frustration that they learned that one of the partners, Moorhouse, had been killed in a car crash. It seemed far too easy a way out for him.

A policeman is at all times a suspicious pragmatist who knows that life is normally far too ragged in operation to clear up after itself: so when a criminal meets a divine justice just before he was due to meet a secular one, he begins to wonder. And when one of two partners, about to be charged with a cruel, vicious fraud, suffers a car accident in which he is burned beyond recognition, and the other partner goes missing, the policeman's suspicions strengthen until, in racing parlance, they become as near certs as any horse can be before it actually passes the post.

The police investigations into the accident began with the car, which belonged to Moorhouse.

It had been coming down a steep hill, clearly marked as such at the top. It had successfully rounded two very sharp bends and then failed to take a third and much easier one. It had ploughed through tube-and-post railing to fall forty-five feet down on rocks, where it had burst into flames and burned violently.

It seemed odd that the car had crashed at the easiest bend. There had been a bottle of whisky in it so the explanation could be that the driver had been drunk and therefore one should not look too hard at any single apparent illogicality, yet ... Only the sidelights had been switched on, although the crash had taken place in the dark. The car had not been in gear and although the experts said that the fall could just conceivably have knocked the gears into neutral, it was a pretty unlikely event ...

The car had burned with a fierceness that had left the interior totally destroyed and the body of the driver charred beyond any immediate recognition. A car which crashes and ruptures its petrol tank can bum very fiercely, but normally the area of complete destruction is localized and beyond that there is very heavy damage but not what the technical experts term 'totality'. On the other hand, soak the interior of the car with petrol before a crash and then there will be totality ...

The police considered the body.

As many a murderer has belatedly discovered, it takes an amazing amount of heat to destroy a body completely, but if a fire is intense enough or the body exposed for long enough, the superficial damage will be so extensive that it will be impossible to identify it solely by visual means.

The dead man had been found lying on the impacted roof – the car had ended upside down – and where his body had been touching the roof small areas of clothing had not been burned to meaningless cinders. From these small areas it had been possible to deduce that the dead man had been wearing light blue pants and a charcoal grey suit. Moorhouse had possessed and had been wearing such clothes that day.

Bonder and Moorhouse were near enough the same height and build, and neither was known to possess any particular deformity. Both men had needed full sets of dentures. And when the remains of those from the corpse were taken to Moorhouse's dentist he checked with his records and said no, they weren't Moorhouse's. On the other hand, when they were taken to Bonder's dentist he said yes, they were Bonder's.

The police discovered footprints leading up the side of the hill from the third bend to above the second one and in one place, where there was a small spring and the ground was very damp, they obtained three very clear shoe-prints. In Moorhouse's bedroom – he lived in a flat: he was separated from his wife – there was a large built-in cupboard in which were a pair of shoes whose patterned soles exactly matched those shoe-prints. Scientific tests confirmed that the dried mud taken from the soles of the shoes was similar in all respects to the earth from around the spring. Moorhouse's daily was asked to check through his clothes and she said that a lot of them were missing. There was no sign of a passport amongst his papers, although one had been issued to him. He had life insurance for fifty thousand pounds, his beneficiary being his wife. And finally he had withdrawn twenty-two thousand pounds from his current account at the Midland Bank two days previously.

The police checked up on Bonder.

None of his clothes was missing, other than those he had been wearing when last seen. His passport was in a cupboard. He had thirty-one thousand pounds in his current account. He had no life insurance. His wife and two children had heard not a word from him. And he had a mistress, twenty-two, pert, very self-possessed, who finally admitted to having in her possession a number of gold coins of Bonder's which she was keeping for him. Mostly Krugerrands, they were valued at just over fifteen thousand pounds.

(As the detective-superintendent in charge of the case had said, the murderer who first thought up a switch of bodies to make it seem he had died had a lot of corpses to answer for).

Accompanying this report there was the letter, signed by the detective-superintendent. At no time during the course of the investigations had the slightest suspicion fallen on Miss Miriam Spiller. However, although there was no reason to believe that she had learned about the fraud before the police began work, equally nothing was known which would prove conclusively that she had not. Consequently, the writer would be grateful if Inspector Alvarez would let him know if it seemed that the death was in some way connected with the events as set out in the report.

Accompanying the letter and the report was a full description of Anthony Moorhouse, three photographs of him, and a copy of the request sent to all foreign police forces, through Interpol, asking them to identify and detain Moorhouse. (Not surprisingly, no such report had ever reached Llueso ...)

The three snapshots were very amateurishly taken and they showed a man with a round, smooth face, a shade too heavy below the cheek-bones, well-built, wearing casual clothes of the kind which did not cost casual money.

'If it seemed that her death was in some way connected with the events' ... The connection surely could not have been more direct. She had been blackmailing Moorhouse.

Chapter Eighteen

Ties hated Alvarez. He tried for the fourth time to knot neatly a blue and red one, then he swore as he untied it and pulled it free. He stamped downstairs. 'Dolores,' he shouted.

She came through from the kitchen, her face reddened from cooking.

'I can't get this bloody thing straight: tie it for me, will you?'

She stared at him. 'Why d'you want to wear a tie in this heat? No one wears one in Celler Tomir.'

'I'm not going there.'

'Then where are you going?'

He hesitated, before finally answering: 'El Mar.'

She arched her eyebrows in exaggerated surprise. 'El Mar! Are you suddenly rich – have you won the lottery?'

'Give over.'

She put her hands on her hips. 'In Celler Tomir, where few tourists go, a thirty-peseta wine costs forty, but in El Mar it costs four hundred. But I suppose you don't care. After all, you will find the food so much better cooked than the food I cook.'

'Of course I won't,' he said feebly.

'I suppose she won't eat where us Mallorquins eat? She wants tablecloths and waiters dressed like penguins who say yes madam, no madam, anything you say, madam.'

'She's not like that.'

'Then why are you going to El Mar?'

'Because I want to.'

'She's bewitched you. You can't mention her without looking like a sixteen-year-old with an ache between his legs.'

'You can stop talking dirty like that,' he snapped.

She sniffed.

'She's nothing like the kind of woman you think she is.'

'Then she's the only foreigner on the island who isn't.' Her manner suddenly changed. 'Oh, Enrique! Haven't you seen them, rushing after our young men like bitches on heat? Haven't you understood what they've done to our youngsters? How many girls do we know who have had to get married in a hurry, carrying their shame up to the altar?'

'You can't blame the foreigners for most of them.'

'Who taught our young to behave like animals? Who destroyed the life we used to know, where there was dignity and honour? Who brought the magazines to our shops with disgusting photographs and words inside which make a decent woman burn with shame?'

He did not answer, because it was all true.

'Give me the tie,' she said wearily. 'When a man becomes hot for a woman, there is no cooling him.' She tied the tie with deft movements, centred it, and patted down the collars of his shirt. As she stepped back, she said: 'If only she had been an islander. Nothing but sadness comes from foreigners.'

'She's more an islander than a foreigner.'

'Have a good meal,' she said dolefully. Her voice strengthened. 'And when you return, you will tell me how much better their cooking is than mine.'

'I'll answer that now: it doesn't compare.'

'Then why are you taking her to a restaurant which only a millionaire can safely enter? Why didn't you bring her here?'

'But you seemed so dead set against her ... '

'Am I a Menorquin gypsy that I'd treat her churlishly? Does she believe me – thanks to what you have told her – some foul-mouthed harridan?'

'Of course not ... '

'Then you are so ashamed of me you dare not bring her here?'

'Mother of God, but you women could twist the Ten Commandments into a devil's liturgy.'

'How else could we ever learn to deal with you men?' she shouted. She put her hands on her hips and stared at him, brown eyes flashing. Then her mood once more changed abruptly. 'Bring her here soon,' she said quietly. 'Then she can decide for herself whether you have cause for shame.'

He drove down to the port and Brenda greeted him with a warm smile. She poured out drinks for them both.

He raised his glass. 'Happiness.' It had become a ritual, private and with special meaning for themselves.

She drank and then said: 'Why so solemn tonight?'

'I'm not really solemn. It's just that my face looks that way when I'm completely relaxed.'

She smiled. 'Happy when sad?'

Or sad when happy? Did he dare yet accept that life was finally offering him compensation for the past?

'You ought to smile more often, Enrique. It changes you.'

'From what and into what?'

She looked at him, her head tilted slightly to one side. 'From a man who expects the worst into one who hopes for the best.'

'Then from now on I shall smile all the time.'

It was impossible to miss the particular inference behind his words and she looked away.

He stood up and took a pack of cigarettes from his pocket to offer her. She accepted one. As he leant over to give her a light, she suddenly smiled.

'What is amusing?' he asked.

'Your tie.' She noticed his expression. 'Don't get upset. Remember, we British proudly admit to having a very peculiar sense of humour. It was the way you twisted your head as you leaned over because the collar was biting into your neck and the look on your face which so plainly said that you wanted to rip the tie off and undo the collar.'

'I hate ties.'

'Then take it off.'

'But if we are going to dinner at El Mar ... '

'Surely you're not worried about what the head waiter will think?'

'He will think nothing because he knows that I know that he underdeclared his income for taxation.'

'The advantages of living in a small community ... I'd much rather see you open-necked.'

He undid the tie and the top button of his shirt and put the tie into his pocket. His fingers touched an envelope. 'That's reminded me. There is something I have to ask you before we go out.' He brought the envelope from his pocket. 'I think you must know all the English who live around here?'

'I probably know them all by sight, yes.'

He opened the flap of the envelope and took out the three photographs of Moorhouse. 'Do you recognize this man?' He handed them to her.

She shook her head. 'No, I don't. Should I?'

'I had hoped you would,' he answered, with sudden glumness. 'He is almost certainly the man who murdered the señorita.'

She shivered as she handed the photographs back to him. 'Put like that, it's horrifying. How do you know who killed her?'

He returned to his seat. 'England has written and told me that the señorita worked as a secretary for a firm in which the partners had been carrying out a fraud. The firm, Beach and Thrush, was selling homes to retired English people who wanted to live on the Peninsula.'

'What name did you say?'

He looked at her, vaguely surprised by the tone of her voice. 'Beach and Thrush – have you heard of them?' She turned to her right as she reached over to an ashtray on the small occasional table and picked it up. 'The name seems familiar.' She tapped the ash from her cigarette into the ashtray. 'I suppose I read about them somewhere.'

'The case will have been reported in all your papers because their crime of swindling the retired was so despicably cruel. Such men have no conscience.'

'And Miriam's murder is connected with them?'

'The answer must surely turn out to be yes. I will not believe Señor Finnister killed her. To kill in cold blood needs courage and determination. But if he did not kill her for money, who else had a motive?

I discovered that although the señorita received money regularly which she said was her pension, it could not have been a pension because Beach and Thrush had become bankrupt and she was not old enough for the state pension. Then there were the two hundred thousand pesetas which she needed so desperately to help the señor ... Where could that money have come from if not from blackmail? She must have known where the surviving partner is living and he was paying her to keep quiet.' 'Surviving partner?'

'Moorhouse had a car crash in which it seemed he was burned to death: there had been a bottle of whisky in the car so perhaps he had been drunk. But the police were suspicious and they discovered that the body belonged to Bonder, not Moorhouse. Moorhouse had murdered him and tried to make it seem it was his own body because then he could escape and no one would ever look for him.

Think about the two deaths of Bonder and the señorita. Both were meant to look like accidents which had been caused by drinking too much. Only because of certain little mistakes did it become obvious in each case that they were murders. If a criminal finds a way of carrying out a crime, he usually goes on using that way ... '

'D'you think Moorhouse is living on this island?'

'I am sure of it and I was hoping you would recognize the photograph. But since you did not ... ' He spoke briskly. 'Enough! Tonight now belongs to pleasure, not work.'

*

When they left the restaurant he began to walk diagonally towards his car, but she stopped him. 'Do you know what I want to do now? Go wading in the sea.'

The moonlight was strong enough to show the astonishment on his face.

She led the way across the pavement and down on to the sand. She took off her shoes. 'When did you last do this? Years and years ago, I'll bet! You've become far too staid and stuffy, so in penance tonight you're going to go for miles and miles.'

There was a recklessness in her now, he thought: the recklessness of youth. Could they both be young again?

'It's a special magical night. So hurry up and take off your shoes and socks and roll up your trousers, just like all the staid and stuffy uncles used to do at Blackpool.'

He wasn't certain he understood her now, but he didn't want to. He took off his shoes and socks, rolled up his trousers, joined the laces of the shoes together and then balanced the shoes across his shoulder. 'I have very knobbly knees.'

She laughed, her head thrown right back. 'Oh, Enrique, how wonderful you are! What a shame that the real you is so often hidden. Come on, hold hands – we can't possibly wade through the sea without holding hands.' Hand in hand, they moved through the luke-warm, moon-sparkling sea. He discovered that indeed it was a special, magical night.

*

On Thursday afternoon, Alvarez returned to his office after a quick lunch, slumped down in his chair, and stared at the scribbled note on his desk. All guardia and municipal police had now reported that no one resembling Anthony Moorhouse was living in their areas. The file photographs of those who had been granted residencias had been checked and none had been of Moorhouse ... Was Moorhouse living off the island and, since the señorita had never left it, had he visited her at the beginning of each month, either flying or arriving by ferry? But passenger lists had been checked with the aid of a computer, as had been immigration cards, and there had been no passenger who had regularly travelled to the island at the beginning of each and every month. Had he cabled her the money or sent it by bank drafts which she had cashed at other banks even though she had no accounts with them? But enquiries had been made and the money had not reached her in this way ... Then he had to be living on the island even if it appeared that he could not be.

Sweet Mary, he thought, but a man could twist his brains into only so many knots before he went mad. He closed his eyes.

The telephone rang, jarring him awake and when, through bleary eyes, he saw the time he wondered who could be so incredibly stupid as to use the telephone at ten to four on a boiling hot summer's afternoon?

Superior Chief Salas could be. What progress had been made in the case? Was Inspector Alvarez at very long last able to state with certainty who had murdered the señorita? Had he arrested the murderer ... ?

Ten minutes later, Alvarez replaced the receiver. The devil take them all: Superior Chief Salas, the captain of the post, and any other hotheads from the Peninsula. He interlaced his fingers and rested them on his stomach. He settled back in the chair. He closed his eyes ...

The internal telephone rang. 'Goddamn it,' he shouted down the receiver, 'can't you read the clock?'

'What are you on about? It's after five.'

He grunted.

'A bloke from the municipal police in Puerto Playa Nueva has just dropped in an envelope for you.'

'All right, I'll come and get it.'

He stood, stretched, and yawned. He ran his tongue around the inside of his mouth and quickly discovered that that had been a mistake. He went over to the shutters and pushed them open and the sunlight burst into the room, like a lance of fire.

Returning from downstairs, he brought from the brown envelope a brief note and four sheets of paper on which were listed the names and addresses of a hundred and twenty-five people. He read through the names and extracted those which were obviously British – Brookes, Tucker, and Cosgrove – who lived in Llueso, Puerto Llueso, or Playa Nueva, and who had been fined for wrongful parking at the beginning of the month.

*

Brookes looked like an advertisement for beer drinking. His round face bloomed, his wattled chin flowed, his paunch rolled.

'Have a drink, Inspector. The grand thing about this place is, there's no yard-arm to worry about ... Don't know if you understand that?'

'I think so,' replied Alvarez, as he sat in the overcrowded sitting-room of the small, boxy bungalow in the hinterland of the large urbanizatiòn at the back of Playa Nueva.

'Now, what's it to be?'

'A little brandy, please.'

The one thing I haven't got!' He boomed with laughter. 'A *little* brandy – never seen one of them in this house.'

Alvarez was served a brandy which even by his standards was large. 'Señor, I am asking questions because of Señorita Spiller.'

'Poor old bitch. Excuse the French,' he added, very hurriedly. 'I didn't mean that nastily. When a person's dead, one doesn't want to be critical. But neither me nor the missus took to her because she was ... Well, vinegary, and we like a good laugh in life. If you can't laugh, what's the point in living?'

'Then you did not see her very often?'

'To put things really frankly, no more often than we had to. It's a small place out here and it's no good being rude to anyone, but when you really don't take to someone then what's the point of pretending that you do?'

'I think that two months ago you parked along the front in the port and were handed a parking ticket?'

'There's one bloke in the local police who spends his time slapping tickets on people. Miserable S.O.D., if you understand Dutch!'

'On that day, did Señorita Spiller come to your car and have a drive with you?'

'She certainly didn't, that's for sure. No, the missus was with me and if I hadn't shut her up something smartish, we'd have both ended up in jail. Can't stand policemen, she can't ... No offence intended.'

'Señor, were you here about two weeks ago?'

'As a matter of fact, we weren't. The missus thought she might have been having a bit of trouble health-wise – you know what women are when they haven't their kids to worry about any longer – and so we went back home for her to have a check-up. Didn't return until the end of last week. There wasn't anything wrong with her, of course, so it gave us a bit of a holiday ... Come on, bottoms up. I mean, the glass of course! There's nothing so lonely as a single drink.'

*

Casa Malindi was high up on the side of the mountain, in the urbanización behind Llueso. It offered a magnificent view over Llueso Bay, but to reach the front patio one had to climb sixty-three steps, mostly cut out of the rock, and by the time Alvarez reached it he was convinced that not even a view of Paradise could be worth such torturous effort. It was only after he had been resting for some time, with the sweat rolling down his face, that he took enough note of his surroundings to realize that the house was shuttered and the patio was empty of any chairs or tables. He swore.

A man, old and bent, came round the far corner of the house and stared at him, squinting against the sharp light. 'It's you,' he finally said in Mallorquin. 'If I'd known that, I wouldn't have bothered to climb down.'

'What are you doing here?'

'Gardening. In rock.' He hawked loudly and spat. 'If they wanted a garden, why didn't they buy a house where there's some soil?'

Alvarez jerked his head in the direction of the house. 'Where's the owner?'

'How should I know?'

'When were they last here?'

'It's been some time now.'

'A couple of weeks?'

'What are you on about? Months.'

Alvarez took the photographs from his pocket and fanned them out to show them to the gardener. 'Is that Señor Tucker?'

'It ain't. The señor's got a face like a pig when you cut its throat for a matanza.'

'Does he come here often?'

'Maybe twice a year for a couple of weeks and then for the rest of the time the house is left empty – when it could be let for hundreds of thousands of pesetas a month.' Alvarez turned and stared out at the land, set as if seen from a low flying aeroplane. If he were right in all he had surmised, now Cosgrove had to be Moorhouse, even if Brenda had not recognized the photograph.

Chapter Nineteen

Marta opened the front door of Ca Na Reta. 'Morning,' said Alvarez. 'How's the family?'

'Victoriano's had a cold, but he's better now.' She chuckled. 'Not that I can get him to agree. You men take illness so seriously.'

'Why not? Look what's at stake! ... Is the señor in?'

'He's by the pool, baking himself black in the sun. Daft, I call it, but there's no accounting for people. Want a word with him, do you?'

'That's right.'

'Come on through, then.'

He stepped out of the shade of the covered patio on to the pool patio. Cosgrove lay on his stomach, on a towel, close to the edge of the tiled pool. Alvarez stared at the mahogany-coloured back, said, 'Señor,' and waited for Anthony Moorhouse to turn over.

Cosgrove rolled over. 'I'm sorry, when I heard your footsteps I thought you were Marta.' He came to his feet in one lithe movement, then stared curiously at Alvarez. 'Is something wrong?'

Bewildered, Alvarez shook his head. Something was very wrong. Cosgrove was not Moorhouse.

'Well, then, how can I help you?'

He pulled himself together. 'I am from the Cuerpo General de Policia, señor.'

'Here, presumably, because of poor Miriam? People have been saying it wasn't an accident after all and that she was murdered, but one's always hearing the most fantastic rumours ... Let's go over there.'

They sat in two of the gaily-coloured patio chairs at the glass-topped cane table.

'Señor, did you know Señorita Spiller?'

'I'd met her, of course: with only a small British community, one meets everyone sooner or later.'

'Were you friendly?'

126

'I certainly wouldn't put it in those terms. You see, we'd practically nothing in common. At the very most, we'd bump into each other a couple of times a month.'

'When did you last speak with her?'

'That's a bit of a facer! I'd say that now it must be a couple of months since I actually spoke to her – as opposed to seeing her across the road and waving.'

'Was that when you met her at Puerto Playa Nueva?'

'I'm afraid you must have things a bit muddled up. I haven't been to Playa Nueva this year. Ghastly place with all those grotty bungalows.'

'I think that you have to be wrong, señor. On the first of June your car was parked along the Front at Puerto Playa Nueva and a municipal policeman issued you with a parking ticket.'

Cosgrove suddenly stood up. 'Hang on a sec, will you?' He was gone for less than a minute and he returned with a pack of cigarettes and a thin gold lighter. 'Are you a slave to this vice?'

'I do smoke, yes.'

Cosgrove pushed the pack across the table before he sat down. 'Going back to what you were saying. Of course you're right, I did get nobbled for parking so I have been to Playa Nueva relatively recently. It just shows how woolly the mind becomes out here! I wasn't parked for a couple of minutes and the policeman sprang out of the undergrowth to present me with a ticket: enthusiasm for the job carried a little too far. Still, it was no good arguing so I paid up smartly to gain the discount.' He pulled the cigarettes back and tapped out one. He snapped open the lighter and held it forward.

Alvarez lit his cigarette. 'And Señorita Spiller was with you when this happened?'

'What makes you suggest that?'

'I have been told it was so.'

'By the policeman?'

'No, señor. He does not remember the happening – perhaps because he is so generous with his parking tickets. It was a friend of the señorita's who saw her getting into your car.'

Cosgrove said easily: 'I'm afraid this friend is way off-beam. I can remember now why I went over to Playa Nueva – a friend had booked a package holiday at a hotel 'way back from the sea and I went there to have a chat. Then when I was returning I stopped on the Front because he was coming over to my place that evening and I wanted to buy a bottle of Ricard, which is his particular poison. Maybe some woman came over to the car and asked something. Or maybe Miriam went over to a car that wasn't mine ... ' He shrugged his shoulders. 'The one thing I know for sure is that Miriam didn't get into my car on that day ... Tell me something: why should it be of any importance whether or not I did see her there?'

Alvarez answered vaguely: 'I am trying to discover everyone she knew.'

'I'd have thought her fiancé could best help you over that – but I suppose you've spoken to him?'

'Yes, I have.'

'Well, I'm sorry I've not been of much use, but I never knew her as anyone other than a very casual acquaintance. But if there's any other way in which I can be of help ... ?'

The hint was not very subtle. Alvarez stood. 'I have just one more thing to ask you, señor, and then I will bother you no longer. Where did you live in England?'

Cosgrove leaned back in his chair and looked up, an amused, almost supercilious expression on his face. 'Being questioned by the police in Spain is obviously akin to applying for a residencia – apart from the relevant facts, you have to give the names of your grandparents, great-grandparents, Uncle Tom Cobbleigh and all ... Back in England, I lived in a village which was called Besham Without. Those who were ignorant of the country or had a weak sense of humour always asked, without fail, without what.'

'Will you tell me whereabouts in England that is?'

'Sussex.'

'Is it near Brighton?'

Cosgrove looked at him with sudden sharpness, then forced a quick smile. 'The locals always claim it's near Worthing, not Brighton, because Brighton bears the connotation of dirty weekends and Besham Without is very staid ... Why did you ask about Brighton?'

It was Alverez's turn to smile. 'It is the only town in Sussex that I have ever heard about, señor.'

Cosgrove accompanied him to the front door. Try as he did, Cosgrove couldn't quite recapture the easy confidence he had shown earlier.

*

Juan and Isabel had been made to wash and then to put on their best clothes. Jaime, blasphemously incredulous, had been made to shave for the second time that day and had then been threatened with ten fates worse than death if he dared go near the brandy bottle. And Dolores, after a whole afternoon spent in the kitchen, went up to her bedroom and brushed her magnificent black hair a hundred and fifty times with the tortoiseshell brush her mother had given her on her wedding day and afterwards stared in the mirror and wished her lustrous dark brown eyes weren't quite so large or her nose quite so sharp. She put on her best dress and swore to herself that not by look, word, or action, should her family disgrace themselves in front of the foreign señora.

When Alvarez introduced Brenda to his family in the front room, he knew a sudden icy panic. They looked, moved, and spoke, as if they were having their photographs taken ...

Brenda chatted in fluent, if accented, Mallorquin and Jaime said in surprise: 'But you speak Mallorquin!'

'What's the point of living in a country and not speaking the language? Don't you have a saying, "The only way of knowing what a rich man thinks is to become a rich man"?'

Juan, with all the sharp authority of eleven years, said: 'You've got it wrong. It's "how a rich man thinks".'

'Juan!' snapped Dolores. 'You ought to know better than to correct the señora.'

'But I'd much rather learn to get it right,' said Brenda. She turned to Juan. 'I'm sure you'd do my Mallorquin a power of good. I'll bet I pronounce some of my words wrongly?'

'All of them,' he replied immediately. Isabel giggled.

Dolores glared at them to try and make them remember their manners.

'You teach me how to speak Mallorquin correctly and I'll teach you how to speak English. Is that a good bargain?' asked Brenda.

Juan decided that the foreign lady wasn't nearly as bad as being made to wash and change his clothes had made him expect. He talked to her about school and the silly mistress from the Peninsula who tried to teach them French, but who spoke Castilian with such an accent that no one could understand her. Isabel chimed in to say that her mathematics teacher stuttered. Jaime relaxed and, pretending not to see the furious look his wife gave him, reached for the brandy bottle.

Dolores, head held high, marched through to the kitchen. All right, so Jaime had been won over by a smile, but then God had made all men fools when it came to a woman's smile: and Juan and Isabel might already be chatting away as if they had known the señora for years, but they were not old enough to be able to judge ... She, at least, was not to be overwhelmed by a smile and she was more than able to judge ...

When they sat down to the meal, there was a tablecloth on the table. To Dolores's horror, Jaime loudly demanded to know if the governor general were coming to eat with them? He then topped that by telling a story which was broad even by Mallorquin standards which concerned a tablecloth, a beautiful young lady, and a great hidalgo. Never again, Dolores dismally told herself, would she be able to hold up her head: her family had disgraced her. Yet, far from sneering at the family's behaviour, Brenda was obviously happy to be amongst them. She told a story, certainly no less broad, about a man who was riding through a forest when he came across a beautiful maiden carrying an ugly frog ...

Jaime could be an amusing host when he felt completely at ease. He had a sharp eye for the ridiculous, a healthy disrespect for affectations, and a peasant's full-blooded joy of life that enabled him to joke about matters which, if said by someone less robustly alive, would have sounded crude and objectionable. By the end of the meal, Dolores was laughing as much as any of them.

*

Alvarez braked the car to a halt in front of the block of flats in the port.

'Thank you for the happiest evening I've had in years.' She briefly laid her hand on his arm. 'I mean that.'

'For me, also, it is the happiest in many, many years.' 'They're a wonderful family, Enrique. Do you think they'd all come and have a meal with me soon?'

'But of course.'

'Even Dolores?'

He smiled. 'Poor Dolores. Until now she has been so certain that she knew what all foreigners were like.'

Brenda opened her door. 'I'd better get moving. I've to be at the airport by six in the morning to meet an incoming flight. I hate the early morning jobs – everyone gets off the plane so very crotchety.'

'If there's ever any trouble ... '

'I know.' She laughed. 'Call for Sir Galahad Alvarez. And an ambulance.'

He escorted her into the building. 'Don't bother to come all the way up,' she said, as she pressed the time switch to bring on the stair lights.

'I'll see you safely into your flat.'

She looked at him for several seconds, then began to climb.

'What are you thinking?' he asked.

'About the two faces of Spain. The kindness and the cruelty: the sunlight and the shadow: the love and the hate.'

They were silent until they reached the third floor. She took a key from her handbag, put it into the lock of the front door, turned it and pushed open the door. As she switched on her hall light, all the stair lights went out. 'Usually the outside ones go off just before I can get to my own door – you must have an influence on them ... The button's to your right.'

He pressed the switch and the stair lights came on once more.

'Good night, Enrique.' She came forward and brushed his cheek with her lips, then went into the flat and closed the door.

He walked down the stairs. Sweet Mary, then a man could be reborn!

When he arrived back at his house, Jaime was in the second room, sprawled out in a chair. 'You cunning old bastard!' he said enthusiastically. 'Fancy finding yourself a bit of crackling that smart.'

'Shut your crude mouth,' said Dolores furiously. 'You don't talk about decent women in such a manner.' She turned. 'Enrique, you are to tell her that from now on our house is her house.' Her tone became haughty. 'If she can bear to share it with a loud-mouthed baboon.'

'It wasn't me who said all foreign women were whores,' Jaime pointed out.

'You're drunk,' she retorted icily.

Jaime grinned as he pushed the bottle of brandy across the table towards Alvarez.

*

Alvarez leaned back in the chair in his office and put his feet on the desk. He stared through the unshuttered, open window at the wall of the house opposite. When facts led irresistibly to a conclusion, which then turned out to be utterly false ...

Perhaps the facts were wrong? But some were demonstrably correct and others must surely be presumed to be correct. For instance, what possible reason could there be for the woman in the library to have been lying? ... Perhaps all the facts were right, but the conclusion he'd drawn from them was at fault. Who – with the possible exception of a psychiatrist – could say for certain that Finnister was incapable of so unambiguous, final a deed as a murder? Emotion could make strong men weak and, more to the point, weak men strong ...

But if the señorita's money had not come from Moorhouse, where had it come from? No other possible source had come to light. And look at the similarities between the two murders. In both, the crime had been set out as an accident. In both, a near-empty bottle had been used to suggest drunkenness. In both, the murderer had used his assessment of the probable course of the police investigation to lead the police off on false scents ...

The murders must have been committed by the same man. Yet, in the obvious fact that Cosgrove was not Moorhouse seemed to lie the proof that they had not been ... But if Cosgrove was in no way connected with the murders, why had he lied about meeting the señorita in Puerto Playa Nueva ... ?

*

They sat at one of the tables of a front café. Brenda, enjoying an iced lemon drink, stared at Alvarez and her forehead creased with lines of worry. 'You look absolutely worn out.'

'To tell the truth, I feel it. My mind's going round and round in ever diminishing circles and it's driving me nuts! ... The same questions getting the same answers, which have to be wrong.'

'Questions and answers about Miriam?'

The tables on either side of them were unoccupied, but he still lowered his voice. 'I was so positive that Cosgrove must be Moorhouse: everything I'd learned said that he had to be.'

'But he isn't.'

'No. He isn't.' He drank some coffee, replaced the cup on a saucer, and then half turned on his chair to stare, squinting, out at the bay, almost as if somewhere amongst that beauty he would find the answer.

'Enrique, it seems ... Well, it seems to have become something personal as far as you're concerned: almost like a crusade. Why?'

'It's my job to identify the murderer. There's nothing more to it than that.'

'Yes, there is.'

He turned back to look into her calm brown eyes. After a while, he said: 'It's the thought of that lonely, unloved woman who'd led a life of monotonous grey until she suddenly thought she'd found a chance of bright colour. That marriage was going to give her all she'd ever longed for. And then, before she reached it, she was murdered. For me, to impose unhappiness is a very great crime.'

'Thank you for telling me,' she said softly.

He showed his astonishment. 'Why do you thank me?'

'Because even though you're a man who hates to bare his soul, you've turned back just a corner of it for me.' She smiled. 'And now I've added to your troubles by making you embarrassed. As my mother would say in moments of exasperation, if only I'd leam to curb my curiosity I'd be a much easier person to have around.' As she finished speaking, she looked at her watch.

'Do you have to leave now?'

'I can squeeze in a few more minutes before I have to discover whether I've a load of trouble at the Pinos because Mrs Brown is still demanding to be flown home as her husband is far too interested in a blonde he met out here on their first day.'

'If she is a woman of any practical sense, she will not leave him with his new friend, the blonde.'

'That's the line I'm taking. Especially as all flights are booked up and she's precious little chance of being able to leave early.'

'What strange holidays some people have!'

'What strange people some people are!' She finished the lemon in her glass. As she replaced the glass on the table, the remaining crushed ice tinkling, she said: 'I wish I knew how they make this. In the really hot weather it's absolute nectar.'

'It contains lemon, sugar, and egg, but I can't say what else. But Dolores is bound to know. Ask her.'

'I'll do that. And maybe one day she'll teach me how to cook some of the local dishes ... Oh, well, I'd better finally get moving and return to work. And don't go on and on beating your head against that brick wall: it can only lead to a terrible headache.'

'But there should be no brick wall there,' he said angrily. 'It is now all so obvious. Yet the obvious is impossible. How can I not keep on hitting my head and getting crazier and crazier ... ' He stopped abruptly. He stared at her, his lugubrious face creased with astonishment. 'But of course! Only a very simple man would not have seen before that when one meets the impossible one does not turn back, one advances.

If the señorita was killed because she was blackmailing someone, that someone is the murderer. If she worked for a firm which committed a great fraud, then the murderer must also have worked for that firm. If the English police say only the two partners were concerned in the fraud, one of those two must be the murderer. If the first partner is dead, murdered by the second one, then the second partner must also have murdered the señorita. But if this is impossible one does not retreat, one advances. To discover that if the second partner did not murder the señorita, then the first one must have done.'

'But aren't you now saying that Blane Cosgrove is Bonder, the partner who was murdered?'

'He has to be,' he replied simply.

Chapter Twenty

Like all truths, thought Alvarez as he drove along the gently rising road to Llueso, this one became blindingly obvious the moment one accepted it.

What the English police had not appreciated was that Bonder had been a razor-keen gambler. Like every other swindler the world had ever known, he had wanted to escape to the life of luxury his swindle would earn him but he could not simply disappear with the money since then an international call would go out and sooner or later, probably sooner, he would be identified and extradited back to England. So his problem had been how to disappear in such a way that the police would not be looking for him.

He was prepared to murder in order to escape. So why not murder Moorhouse, stage an 'accident', and set the scene to make it appear that the body was, in fact, his own? Then he would be 'dead' and it would be assumed that Moorhouse had taken off with all the money. The police forces in all countries would be looking for Anthony Moorhouse and not Colin Bonder ... There were two serious drawbacks to this solution. The idea was not an original one, and the police weren't fools. If the body was unrecognizable through burning, the police were going to think that it was an odd coincidence that this 'accident' should happen just when they had been about to arrest both men for fraud. They would be suspecting a switch of bodies even before seriously beginning to investigate. That meant that the odds against fooling them into believing the dead man was himself and not Moorhouse were very slight ... But what if he introduced a double switch? Used the certainty of the police's suspicions to make them believe the lie ... ?

Let it be seen to be Moorhouse who staged the 'accident' and switched bodies, trying to escape justice through being declared dead. Then it would be his car and his clothes which would be involved. The police would start by suspecting that it was he who had murdered Bonder and switched bodies. Supply a vital piece of evidence to support their belief – the teeth. Supply back-up evidence – a large sum of money withdrawn from Moorhouse's account only a day or two before (what pretext had Bonder used to persuade Moorhouse to withdraw this money?), footprints made by his shoes found in his bedroom cupboard, clothes and passport missing ... While in order to establish Bonder's death the large sum of money left untouched in the bank and the gold coins with the mistress (forty-six thousand pounds sacrificed in order to preserve several hundreds of thousands: good odds for the gambler), and the passport amongst his papers ...

Alvarez turned off the road on to the dirt track. A moment later, he parked in front of Ca Na Reta.

Marta opened the front door. 'You again?' Her eyes lit up with inquisitive interest.

'I just want another brief word with the señor.'

'Well, you're out of luck. He's not in. Went to the village to pick up his mail and then he's off for the day with one of his women.'

Alvarez scratched his neck. 'Has he many women?'

'With his money? He rustles the notes and they come running.' She laughed shrilly. 'Not that chasing his money has done one of 'em much good.'

'How d'you mean?'

'Her belly began to grow so she came up here, begging him to marry her. The silly young fool didn't even know what kind of a man she'd been bedding with.'

'He wouldn't play?'

'What do you think?'

'It's a great life for the rich.'

'It's a great life for you men, rich or poor. You have your fun and away while us women have to stay and nurse the trouble.'

He said goodbye and returned down the steps. He reached his car and was about to climb in behind the wheel when he heard the crunching of a car's tyres on the dirt track. He waited and soon a green Seat 132 turned into the drive. Cosgrove was at the wheel and by his side was an extravagantly beautiful brunette. He parked alongside the battered Seat 600 and climbed out. 'What's brought you back here?' he asked, trying to sound polite, but failing.

'There are a few more questions I need to ask you, señor.'

'I've told you all I know. And in any case, I'm in a hurry to get away. I've only called back to pick up my camera, which I forgot.'

'Nevertheless, I should be grateful if you would help me.'

Cosgrove nodded curtly. 'Five minutes at the most.' He returned to the car and said to the brunette: 'Sorry about things, Gilly, but I must have a quick word with this bloke – he's a detective. We'd better go into the house.'

Gillian climbed out of the car. She stared briefly at Alvarez, then crossed to the steps and climbed them. She was wearing a see-through blouse and no brassiere and her blood-red slacks were tightly cut so that they hugged her shapely buttocks. Cosgrove opened the door for her and she swept through, petulantly upset by this change of plan. She went out to the pool.

As soon as they were alone in the sitting-room, Cosgrove said: 'Well, what is it now?'

'Señor, when you lived in England, did you work for a firm called Beach and Thrush?'

He was so shocked that for the moment he could only stare at Alvarez.

'And was your name then Colin Bonder?'

He finally managed to regain some measure of composure. 'Of course it wasn't.'

'Señor, if Bonder is your true name, it will save very much trouble if you tell me so now.'

'My name's Cosgrove and always has been. God knows what ridiculous ... '

He was interrupted by a call from outside. 'Hurry up, darling. It's bloody boring out here.'

They looked through the french windows. The sharp sunlight outlined Gillian's breasts through the light green blouse, a fact of which, to judge from her careful pose, she was fully aware.

'I won't be long,' he called back, his voice hoarse.

'At least you might give me a drink.'

'I'll send Marta out with one.' He gratefully took the chance to leave the room. He returned after a minute and Marta, carrying a silver tray with a glass on it, accompanied him. She went out and handed the glass to Gillian and then returned round the outside of the house to the kitchen.

Cosgrove said, trying to sound his usual confident, ironic self: 'I must commend your imagination, if not your accuracy.'

'Señor, you are Colin Bonder.'

'The name is Blane Cosgrove. It's Blane because my parents never consulted me and ... '

'Since you do not wish to make things easy I must now ask you to bring me your passport and your residencia.'

'Why?'

'Because if I have the passport you cannot leave: and since the residencia contains your photograph and one of your fingerprints, when I send it to England it will help them to tell me the truth.'

Cosgrove looked as if he had been hit.

Gillian petulantly called out: 'Aren't we ever leaving?'

'Have another drink,' he managed to answer.

'High living!'

Cosgrove turned to face Alvarez. 'Are you rich?' he asked harshly.

'I am a poor man, señor.'

'All right. Then tell me how much England knows at the moment?'

'Very little. Until this morning, I also knew very little.'

'What would happen if you didn't send them my residencia?'

'They would undoubtedly continue to believe that Señor Bonder is dead, while Señor Moorhouse is alive.'

'Suppose I give you ... ten million pesetas?'

A house, carefully renovated, ready for her: thousands of square metres of irrigated land to bear olives, almonds, figs, oranges, lemons, quinces, algarrobas, peppers, aubergines, lettuces, tomatoes, beans, cabbages, cauliflowers, carrots, radishes, sweet potatoes, artichokes ... 'It'll be in cash. No one can ever know.'

He spoke gravely. 'I am sure that in your country, just as here, it is a serious crime to try to bribe a policeman.'

'All right. Fifteen million.'

Both of them had become so involved that they had no idea Gillian had left the pool-side and entered the sitting-room, until she said, in her careless, drawling voice: 'So where's my drink? Still being distilled?'

'Get out,' said Cosgrove wildly. 'Get out of here, you stupid bitch.'

'I'm not having you call me stupid! If that's how you feel, you can drive me straight back to my flat.' She waited, but when he ignored her she crossed through to the hall, slammed open the door, and went outside. 'Your passport and residencia, please.'

Cosgrove stared at Alvarez, then left the room. When he returned, he said in tones of angry bewilderment: 'Why haven't you the sense to take the money?'

How did one describe colour to a blind man?

*

Alvarez was drinking his morning cup of coffee on Saturday when the telephone rang. Juan answered it and returned to the kitchen. 'It's for you, Uncle. Someone at the post wants you urgently.'

He tore off a piece of bread, dunked it in the coffee, and ate it, before slowly walking through to the front room and the telephone.

'Get down to the port right away,' snapped the captain. 'One of the fishing-boats has brought in a motor-cruiser found at sea with no one aboard. It belongs to Cosgrove.'

Chapter Twenty-One

Moremo was small and gnarled, with a skin made leathery by sun, sea, and wind, and the far-seeing eyes of a man who was often staring at distant horizons. He lifted up the last wooden box of fish and handed it to his companion, then rubbed his scale-covered hands down the sides of the dungarees he was wearing. 'Most of the night out beyond the bay and no more'n five boxes of cheap fish to show for it.'

'It's not as it used to be,' said Alvarez.

'When I was a kid, we'd come back with more fish in one night than now we get in a week. But you know what? In them days, we got only a few pesetas a box.'

'So nothing's really changed.'

He looked beyond his time-scarred boat, with its single rickety wheelhouse set aft of the stubby mast, at the far side of the harbour where the luxury yachts and motor-cruisers lay. 'For some it hasn't: for others it has.'

Calbò, a mute with a face alive with fun, jumped down from the quay on to the boat. 'Wash her down,' said Moremo. Calbò nodded, picked up a wooden bucket with a line attached, and threw the bucket over the side to scoop up water which he used to sluice down the deck before he began to scrub it with a long-handled broom.

Moremo led the way for'd and climbed up on to the quay. A Citroen CX passed as Alvarez joined him. 'She's up here.' He turned and walked, with the shuffling gait which came from having spent so much time aboard small boats whose movements could never be accurately pre-judged. 'We weren't doing no good so I said to Leandro, it's fine, the sea's calm, and if I can read a night sky it's staying that way, so let's sail further out. We didn't catch nothing there either.'

He came to a halt by a smart, seaworthy motor-cruiser, made fast by her stern to the quay between a ketch and a far larger and more luxurious motor-cruiser.

He studied her. 'There should be some salvage for me and Leandro. I'd say there was twelve or fifteen million floating there.' His tone of voice suggested that he would not be too surprised if it finally turned out that they were not entitled to salvage money.

A small gangway with rope handrails had been rigged between the stern and the quay, and they boarded. 'She'd manage a fair sea,' said Moremo. 'Not like that there.' He hawked and spat in the direction of the much larger motor-cruiser alongside. 'Sail her into any kind of a sea and with so much superstructure she'd turn turtle.' Alvarez took a pack of cigarettes from his pocket and offered it. 'Let's hear about how you found this boat.' He flicked open his lighter.

Moremo drew the smoke deep into his lungs and immediately coughed heavily. 'The old woman's always on at me to see the quack over me cough. I keep telling her, if it's nothing, it's too soon; if it's something, it's too late ... ' He shifted, to move into the shade thrown by the flying bridge. 'Like I was saying, we was well out beyond the heads and doing no good and then come the dawn and I saw her, out beyond us. Didn't take much notice to begin with until I realized she was steaming in circles. I said to Leandro, let's go and see if her steering gear's broken down: could be good for a few thousand pesetas to tow the silly bastards into harbour.

We came in close and I gave a hail and there wasn't no answer. I drew alongside – she wasn't steaming fast – and Leandro boarded. He had a look round and signalled there wasn't no one aboard. I got him to stop the engines and then he returned to our boat and I boarded this one to see for myself. After that, we brought her in.'

'Did you know she came from here?'

'Of course,' he answered scornfully, surprised he should be asked such a question. He knew and could describe every boat which sailed into or out of the harbour.

'Did you touch anything?'

He blew his nose with his fingers.

'Come on, you old bastard. What were you at?'

'There was a bottle of whisky on the table in the saloon.'

'So you poured yourself a drink? How much was in the bottle before you started?'

'It were less than half full. Much less,' he added, by way of insurance.

'Have you any idea of what happened out there?'

'The owner fell over the side, didn't he?'

'What makes you so certain?'

Moremo didn't answer directly, but walked across to the port side and then aft. He stopped two-thirds of the way along the after deck and pointed at the stanchions, slotted into the deck, through which rope was reeved to form rails: one of the stanchions had pulled loose and was lying cater-cornered, held at an angle of forty degrees by the tension of the ropes. 'Slipped on the grease and went overboard,' he said.

There was an irregular patch of brown grease on the otherwise clean deck and something had scraped through this grease in the direction of the side of the hull.

'They think they can leave a boat to look after herself while they booze themselves silly.'

Alvarez thought for a moment and then asked: 'Suppose the owner fell overboard where you saw this boat. Where's his body going to end up?'

'All depends, don't it? Get a strong southerly and maybe it heads straight into the bay.'

'But surely we don't usually get strong winds at this time of the year and even if we do it's more likely to be a northerly?'

Moremo flipped the butt of his cigarette over the side. 'If you know that much, you're a bloody sight cleverer'n me.'

Alvarez smiled. 'All right, so anything can happen! But what if we don't get any strong winds?'

'It'll like as not miss the island.'

'And how long d'you reckon it'll last in the water?'

'When I was a nipper one of me dad's shipmates went missing in a freak storm in early summer. The body was sighted three weeks later and the only way they could tell it was him was because he'd lost half an arm a couple of years earlier when a derrick fell on it ... This bloke was a rich foreigner, weren't he?' Moremo went on. 'Always having women aboard. Women and the sea don't mix and never did.'

'You'd have jumped at the chance to mix 'em when you were young.'

'I'm not so old I wouldn't know what to do now, but I'd not be the fool to do it at sea,' he retorted sharply. 'Have you finished? I need to be getting back to work.'

'Just before that, are you sure the bottle of whisky was more than half empty before you started on it?'

'That's what I said, ain't it?'

'Were there any glasses?'

'There was the one on the table.'

'Did you use it?'

'What for? There was the bottle, wasn't there?' Moremo waited a moment, then made his way aft to the gangplank and went ashore.

Alvarez entered the accommodation. There were two cabins, one considerably larger than the other, one shower-room, heads, galley, and large saloon.

The double bunk in the larger cabin was made up and clothes were hanging in the wardrobe which was built against the for'd bulkhead. By the side of the cupboard was a small desk and in this was a passport with a photograph of Cosgrove in the name of Thomas Holmes which bore several entry and exit stamps for French, Italian, and Spanish ports, 116,000 pesetas and £541 in notes, registration papers for the boat made out in the name of *Sheelagh III* (At the moment she was *Esther* C), a letter from the Banque du Commerce in Geneva, addressed to Monsieur Holmes, confirming that the requested account had been opened and that in order to have money transferred it was necessary to give the name of the transferee, to quote the number already designated, and to provide a signature, and a couple of letters addressed to Thomas Holmes, signed by Claudia, which were written in unambiguously passionate terms.

He searched the second cabin, which proved to be empty of everything other than bed-clothes, and then went through to the galley. The tiny refrigerator was filled with perishable food, including eggs, butter, milk, and half a litre of cream in a plastic container. The store cupboards contained a wide selection of tinned goods and also three loaves of bread. In the vegetable rack were potatoes, tomatoes, red peppers, grapes, and apples.

The table in the saloon was on the starboard forward bulkhead and on this, in a fiddle container, were a bottle of whisky, now less than a fifth full, and a glass.

He sat down on the bench seat running along the hull and stared at the whisky. Cosgrove was a clever man, clever enough to have realized that some day his cover might be blown and he would be identified as Colin Bonder. So from the beginning he had been ready to make a quick get-away if the need ever arose: false papers for himself and for his boat, and the bulk of his money in Switzerland, in a numbered account. Then if it became necessary, all he had to do was to steam out of the port and make for France, arriving with a different name and a different boat ... The alarm had sounded and he had sailed out of the port. Then, suddenly, his plans had gone dramatically wrong. Walking along the deck, with several whiskies under his belt to slow down his reactions, he had trodden on some grease, slipped, and fallen against the rails. Because he was a landlubber and had failed to keep a trim eye on his craft, one of the stanchions had been almost out of its socket and the force of his body hitting the rope rails had jerked it right out, and the impetus of his fall had taken him over the side. When he had surfaced, the boat had been several metres away, steaming too fast for there to be the slightest chance of his ever catching up with her ... Justice had finally, if belatedly, caught up with him.

He lit a cigarette and then, rather absentmindedly, poured himself a whisky. It was a neat ending to a nasty case. He drank. He drew on the cigarette and let the smoke trickle out through his nostrils. Too neat an ending?

Boats could change their names, but not their silhouettes: a man could change his name, but not his main physical characteristics. If Cosgrove had disappeared with his boat, everywhere in the Mediterranean would have been on the alert. Into whichever port he had sailed as Thomas Holmes, owner of *Sheelagh III*, there would surely have been someone curious to know if, by chance, his real name were Blane Cosgrove and the boat's were *Esther C* ... ?

So, to a man with a mind like a bent corkscrew, it would obviously be far safer to fake his own death – wasn't he now an expert at this sort of thing? – and then to double back on his tracks, land on the island with a third identity, and catch a plane to another part of Europe long before the local detective had begun to foresee such a possibility ...

He drained the glass, left the saloon, and made his way ashore. He walked back down the quay to the fishing boats. Moremo and Calbò were now mending a net and Alvarez sat down on a handy iron bollard, but hurriedly stood up when the heat reached through his trousers to scorch his flesh.

The two fishermen laughed. Moremo said scornfully: 'So it's not just the foreigners who are soft!'

'Mother of God, but that was a hot seat! ... I need to know something more. Did that motor-cruiser normally ever carry any sort of a tender?'

Moremo worked his shuttle with a deftness which made it all look easy. 'Aye, she did.'

'What kind?'

'An inflatable with an outboard.'

'And this wasn't aboard?'

'If it had been, it'd still be there now.' He looked up, but continued to work the shuttle. 'It never hurt no one to lose a drop of whisky, but taking a tender would be stealing.'

Alvarez was satisfied that the tender had been missing when they first boarded the boat.

*

The receptionist at the Hotel Pinos told Alvarez that Señora Stewart had telephoned early that morning to say she was not feeling well and wouldn't be at work, at least before midday. This sent him racing to her flat, imagining a whole series of terminal illnesses. To his great relief, however, it became clear it was not that severe when, dressed, she opened the front door of her flat.

'They told me at the hotel you were ill,' he said, breathless after his too hurried climb up the stairs.

'It's just that I woke up with a cracking head,' she Said dully.

'Have you called the doctor?'

'No.'

'Then I'd better ... '

'For God's sake, stop fussing.'

He showed his hurt.

She tried to speak more calmly. 'I'm sorry, Enrique, I didn't mean to snap like that ... Come on in and I'll make some coffee.'

He entered. 'Why have you got a bad headache?'

'There's no cause for alarm. I suffer them every now and then – it's one of the penalties of being born a woman.' She spoke lightly for the first time. 'There's no sex equality when it comes to headaches. But forget it – I've dosed myself, so it'll disappear sooner or later.'

He followed her into the kitchen and watched her half-fill the kettle and put it on the gas-stove.

'Has anything in particular brought you down to the port?' she asked, as she put two mugs down on a worktop.

'Something very important.'

She opened a cupboard and brought out a china sugar-bowl. 'Such as?'

'Two fishermen have found a motor-cruiser out at sea going round in circles with no one aboard. She belongs to Blane Cosgrove.'

He waited for her to say something, but she crossed to the refrigerator, opened it, and brought out a plastic bottle of milk. 'It seems he fell over the side and drowned.'

'Poor devil,' she said.

'The boat was towed into harbour and I've just come from searching her. It looks as if he had been escaping, under a false name, before I had enough evidence to arrest him. Unfortunately for him he'd been drinking and he slid on a patch of grease, came hard up against a stanchion which was loose, didn't react quickly enough because of the alcohol, and went over the side.'

She spooned instant coffee into the mugs. 'You sound as if you think something's wrong with that?'

'It's all too pat. I don't believe he is dead.'

She carried the jar of coffee back to the store cupboard.

'Do you remember what I told you about the two murders? The way in which an attempt was made to conceal the truth under the guise of accidents brought on by heavy drinking? It's precisely the same pattern here. An accident, a three-parts-empty bottle of whisky on the table in the saloon ... The tender's missing. I've checked, and his boat always carried an inflatable with an outboard.'

The kettle began to boil. She switched off the gas and carried the kettle to the table to pour water into the mugs.

'I reckon he set the scene to make me believe he'd been intending to break free in the boat, but in fact he never intended any such thing. He returned ashore in the tender, sank it, made his way to Palma airport, and under a third identity flew off this morning by the first plane which could take him. By now, he could be virtually anywhere in Europe.'

'What are you going to do?' She returned the kettle to the stove.

'Get on to Interpol and ask for an All Countries Search. But the chances of catching him ... ' He shrugged his shoulders.

'Help yourself to sugar and milk.'

He took two spoonfuls of sugar and added quite a lot of milk.

'Enrique ... ' She became silent.

He looked up. Her face was strained as she came and stood immediately next to him and helped herself to milk and sugar. 'Let's go through to the sitting-room,' she said.

They went through and she immediately settled in one of the armchairs. She closed her eyes. 'There's something you've got to know, Enrique. I had to work really late last night and by the time I'd managed to settle everyone in the hotels, I was so dog-tired I wasn't tired any more – if you know how I mean. So I went for a walk along the front to try and ease off.' She stopped.

He sipped the coffee.

'I saw Blane leave harbour in his boat.'

'Are you certain it was him?'

'It was his boat – I've always liked the look of her because she's much more seaworthy than so many of the floating gin-palaces in the port ... I've never told you, have I, that Gerry was an enthusiastic weekend sailor?'

'No, you haven't.'

'His great love was sailing and I used to crew for him. It's odd, but afloat he changed completely and became quite dictatorial, a real ship's skipper. To hear him go for me when he thought I'd done something wrong ... And yet ashore he never once said a really cross word to me ... 'He watched her face, now sad as well as drawn.

'He wasn't on his own when he sailed.'

'What?'

She opened her eyes and looked straight at him. 'There was another person aboard with him.'

Chapter Twenty-Two

'That's impossible!' Alvarez said, with certainty.

She closed her eyes again. 'They were on the flying bridge.'

'You have to be mistaken. Either it wasn't his boat or else there was something on the bridge which at night looked like a second person.'

'It was Blane's boat, and there were two people on the flying bridge when she left port.'

'But the whole purpose of his plan was to disappear completely: if he took someone with him, there would always be the risk that his new identity would be betrayed.'

She made no answer.

'Did you recognize the second man?'

'She was a woman. I never saw her face.'

Gradually he accepted the fact that she had not been mistaken. Then this had not been Cosgrove's escape trip, but a brief sail to make certain everything was in running order. And because he could not leave the women alone he had taken one along with him ... But when Moremo had boarded there had been no one aboard, and the tender had been missing ...

The missing tender, the bottle of whisky, the patch of grease, the displaced stanchion ... Surely these were meant to paint a now familiar pattern of accidental death, brought about largely by drinking too much. A pattern which in previous cases had turned out to be murder ...

Could this, ironically, have been a genuine accident? Then why had the woman aboard not reported it? Had she died as well, making it a double accident? But why should she have taken to the tender to search for Cosgrove? Or, by the time she had found him in the sea, had he been too weak to climb aboard the boat, and as she couldn't heave him up, had she launched the tender and then missed her footing? ... But the boat had been under power when found by Moremo, and before launching the tender wouldn't she have stopped the engines? ... And two accidental deaths following two murders made to look like accidents ... ?

'Enrique, I'm sorry, but my head is beginning to feel as if two sledge-hammers are at work inside it instead of just one. I must lie down in a dark room.'

He immediately stood. 'I'm terribly sorry. I've been sitting here, not thinking of you but only of what you have just told me.'

She slowly stood and then crossed to grip his two arms. She kissed him, almost violently, rested her cheek against his. 'Enrique ... '

'Brenda, beloved ... '

'Please go. By tomorrow I'll be quite all right.'

He said goodbye and left, and as he walked down the first flight of stairs he ran his fingertips along his cheek and across his lips.

*

Alvarez sat behind his desk and stared at the shuttered window which projected a pattern of light and shade on to the ceiling. After a while he shook his head and picked up the internal phone. 'Has there been any report through of a woman missing?'

'No, nothing like that. But there is something in from England for you – phoned through from Palma when you were out.'

'What's it all about?'

There was a short pause and then the guard read out the report. London said that the photograph and finger print identified Blane Cosgrove as Colin Bonder. Would Inspector Alvarez please forward full details of the case? For their part, England would be sending an interim request to detain Colin Bonder, sometime known as Blane Cosgrove, pending a detailed request for extradition on the grounds of fraud and murder.

He thanked the guard and replaced the receiver. He had been right. But there seemed to be small merit in that because now he was surely once more facing the impossible?

*

He parked his Seat in front of Finnister's flat and climbed the squeaky stairs to the patio. The shutters were closed over the window and the inside curtain was drawn across the glass door. He knocked on the door. There was no answer. He knocked again and called out: 'It's Inspector Alvarez.'

After a while the curtain was drawn back just far enough for Finnister to look out. 'Perhaps, señor, you would open the door?'

Finnister came round the curtain, making certain it did not pull back, unlocked the door and held it partially open. 'What d'you want?'

'That will take a little time to explain so perhaps I may come inside?'

'No, you can't.'

'Señor, let me assure you that there are times when a policeman knows how to be blind.'

'I don't know what on earth you're talking about.'

'For God's sake, Frank, stop being so bloody silly,' Carol called out. 'He's not going to believe you've been spending the last hour writing poetry.'

Slowly, very unwillingly, Finnister pulled the curtain right back and opened the door fully. Alvarez stepped into the room. Carol was doing up the front buttons of her dress: her hair was tangled, her make-up smudged, her face flushed, and her eyes were moist with pleasure.

'My Gawd, but you created panic stations! Frank heard the steps creaking and reckoned it was Ted, and he was under the settee quicker than the sound barrier.'

'I am sorry to have caused so much trouble,' said Alvarez.

'Well, it's not really your fault, is it? ... Frank, how about some drinks all round? I don't know about anyone else, but I need one. Had to dress so quickly I was all thumbs. Tell you what – now I know what gets my knickers in a twist!' She laughed boisterously.

'You mustn't talk like that,' protested Finnister.

'Why the hell not? When I'm with friends?' She turned, to face Alvarez. 'You are a friend, aren't you?'

'Señora, I hope so. I am here to find out.'

She looked at him and the fun drained away from her face. She went over to the rumpled bed, pulled up the sheet and the cover, smoothed the cover down, and then sat on the bed, her legs underneath herself. 'Frank, you're forgetting them drinks.'

Finnister searched for and eventually found an unopened bottle of wine. He tore off the metal cap, pulled out the plastic stopper which he threw on to the table where it lay amongst the debris, and filled three glasses.

Alvarez removed some rubbish from a dining-room chair and sat. 'Did you both know Señor Cosgrove?'

She said: 'Who?'

'Señor Blane Cosgrove, who lived at Ca Na Reta in Llueso.'

'Never heard of him.'

'And you, señor?'

Finnister handed round the glasses and drank heavily from his own before answering. 'I've met him.'

'Was he a friend?'

'Hardly.'

'Why are you on about this bloke?' she asked.

'It seems that he took his motor-boat out to sea last night and at some time he fell over the side. There was a lady with him when the boat sailed and so I wish to speak with her.'

Finnister said, his tone querulous: 'If there was a woman aboard when he fell over the side and drowned, she'd have tried to save him and then have reported what happened.'

'Indeed, señor. But as no one has made such a report I now have to ask myself if perhaps he did not fall, but was pushed by her.'

'Murdered him – and you were asking me if I know him ... ' Carol began to speak wildly. 'You don't think it was me? I told you, I've never met him. Why are you keeping on and on at us? First it was Frank with Miriam and now it's me with someone I don't even know ... '

'Unfortunately, it is my job. Señora, will you please tell me where you were last night?'

She looked at Finnister. He cleared his throat. 'You'll have to tell him,' he finally muttered.

'Look, mister, it's like this.' She looked at Finnister again, but he carefully offered her no support, so she went on very quickly. 'I tried and tried. There ain't no one can say I didn't try.'

'I regret that I do not understand,' said Alvarez.

'I'm on about keeping Ted off his boozing. Ever since we was married and I discovered that when he said he liked a pint he meant a gallon, I've been trying to get him to stop boozing so he could become a man. I've hid his booze and been knocked black and blue because I tried not to tell him where it was ... Then the other day ... Well, Frank turned up at the house, unexpected like, and I had to do something to keep Ted quiet so I gave him a bottle of brandy I'd been hiding from him. That got me to thinking that I was knocking my head against a bloody concrete wall and if I'd any sense I'd stop doing that and help Ted get pig-drunk each night so as I could get away and be with Frank ... It's not as if I hadn't tried for years all I knew ... '

Alvarez tried not to sound slightly shocked. 'Then what happened last night, señora?'

'Frank and me went to the new discotheque at Playa Nueva.'

The thought of Finnister at a discotheque was so incredible that Alvarez immediately believed it. 'Will you tell me at what time you arrived there?'

'It was getting a bit late because Ted was ... Well, he was being bloody difficult. I mean, normally you put a bottle within smelling distance and it's empty a couple of minutes later, but I left a bottle of Soberano in full view and would he start his boozing? Wanted to watch the telly! And him not understanding any more Spanish than uno coñac, dos coñacs, tres coñacs ... I began to think that maybe he suspected what was on ... '

'You think he knows something?' demanded Finnister wildly.

'Gawd, men! We take all the risks and they do all the shivering ... He didn't suspect anything, Frank, he was just being his usual bloody awkward self without realizing it. Still, he started his boozing later on and by ten he was too pig-drunk to know whether it was me or a pink elephant that was in the flat with him.'

'And you came straight here and then on to the discotheque?'

'Up to a point. Only Frank had worked himself into a state because I was late and I had to calm him down and one thing led to another ... D'you understand?'

'I understand, señora. So at what time did you arrive at the discotheque?'

'It must have been a bit after eleven.'

'And when did you leave?'

'Not until after two.'

'Do you think there will be someone there who will remember you?'

She giggled. 'There's one of the DJs fancies himself no end and dances with the customers. He's got three hands so if you're holding on to two, he's still in there, grabbing.'

'Did you dance with him?'

'A couple of times.'

'Six times,' snapped Finnister.

'You get so ratty, Frank,' she said happily. 'You ought to have seen him, mister, standing around, looking like murder ... Oh, my God, I shouldn't have said that, should I?'

'There is no cause to worry. I understand how you meant it.' Alvarez finished his wine and stood. 'Señora, I will have to ask this man with whom you danced, of course, but I am sure that he will confirm what you have told me. So it is certain that you cannot help me over the death of Señor Cosgrove.' He paused, then spoke to Finnister. 'And, señor, I am satisfied you cannot help me over the death of Señorita Spiller.'

She said, her voice rising: 'You don't any longer think he killed her?'

'I do not.'

'Oh, my God, I'm going to cry.' She did so, with spontaneous generosity, and as the tears flowed she jumped off the bed and rushed to Finnister to engulf him.

Alvarez said goodbye. They might not have heard him except that as he opened the door and stepped out on to the patio and into the burning sunshine, he heard a muffled voice saying: 'D'you think Shakespeare could have begun to write Hamlet if he'd been persecuted every minute of his life ... ?'

*

When Alvarez arrived at Ca Na Reta, Marta, who had been cleaning the tiles of the covered patio with gas-oil, said: 'The señor's not here and what's more his bed wasn't slept in. I suppose he's out with one of his women so there's no saying when he'll be back.'

'I am afraid he may not be coming back.'

She carefully put the mop into the gas-oil in the plastic bucket, then squeezed out the excess oil on the grating fixed to the rim. 'How d'you mean, Enrique? Why shouldn't he be coming back?'

'He went out in his boat last night and fell over the side. Or was pushed.'

She had been about to mop a section of tiles. She held the mop out at full stretch as she said: 'Pushed?'

'He may have been murdered.'

'Sweet Mary, preserve me!' she exclaimed.

'So I've come along now to find out if you can help me.'

'But I don't know anything about murdering him.'

'Of course you don't. But you may know something which will help me discover who did kill him. When he sailed out of the port he had a woman aboard and it seems likely she could help a lot. Can you think of any woman who had a reason to dislike him?'

'Any one who knew him,' she answered immediately. She resumed her work and mopped the tiles in front of her.

'But are there any you can be certain particularly disliked him?'

She soaked the mop again. 'There were a couple.' She told him, with a wealth of gossipy detail, what their names were.

*

Gina Yearling shared a tiny flat with another English woman, older than she, who worked for one of the estate agents in the port. When Alvarez told her what had happened, she began to cry.

'Señorita, I am afraid that I must ask you questions. Some of them you will not like, so please believe me that I only ask them because I have to.'

She lit a cigarette with hands which trembled.

'Is it true that you went to his house and told him you were pregnant?'

'How did you know ... ?' She slumped deeper into the chair. 'I suppose it was his daily told you? He always says she understands far more English than she ever lets on because she loves listening in to everything everyone says.'

'Is it correct that you are pregnant?'

'Yes.'

'And he was the father?'

'He's the father. But he'll never ever believe that no one else can be.' There was a hysterical note to the way in which she so determinedly spoke about Cosgrove in the present tense.

'Did you expect him to marry you?'

She drew on the cigarette, then fiddled with it. 'I've knocked around enough so I ought to have learned the score, but when I met him it was like I was fifteen again and I dreamed ... Christ, I dreamed!'

'What did he say when you told him you were pregnant?'

'He offered me five hundred quid and all expenses to go back to England for an abortion.'

'Did you refuse?'

'It's ... it's against my religion. But he can't understand that. It's all so simple for him. You get preggers, you get the trouble scraped out, so what's all the fuss?'

'You wanted to bear his child?'

'Of course I did.' She stubbed out the cigarette in an ashtray. 'Haven't I just told you, I love him.'

'When he refused to marry you, or to do anything but pay for an abortion you wouldn't have, did you not begin to hate him?'

She stared at him, visibly shocked. 'Haven't you understood a single word I've been saying? I can't hate him, I love him.'

'Señorita,' he said quietly, 'I have understood every word you have said and some which you have not. So now I will leave you.'

She lit another cigarette.

'There are times when one desperately needs a friend to help. Tell me where I may find someone to ask her to be here to be with you.'

'There's only Eileen,' she answered dully. 'She shares the flat with me. You don't ... You don't have many friends when you move around a lot.'

'Where will I find her?'

'At the estate agents on the corner of the Parelona road. But her boss is a real slave-driver and won't let her out at this time of the day.'

'I know her employer, Señorita, and I can be certain that he will allow her to come back to be here with you.' She looked up at him and as more tears fell, she said: 'Couldn't ... couldn't he still be alive?'

Sadly, he shook his head.

*

Alvarez parked in the drive of Ca'n Blat, alongside four other very much larger and newer cars. He crossed to the porch and the wooden front door, panelled in a traditional pattern, and rang the bell. A maid, in neat uniform with a scrap of lace perched jauntily on her head, opened the door. He said he wanted to have a word with the señora.

'But she's people in for drinks. You couldn't come back some other time ... ?' Seeing him shake his head, she sighed. 'All right, come on in and I'll tell her. But don't blame me if she gets in a right state over it!'

He was shown into the small sitting-room, obviously seldom used, which contained several pieces of antique furniture that even to his uninformed eyes were of great quality. Agnes – a red-head with a heavy fringe which nearly reached her eyes – came into the room, her expression one of wealthy annoyance. 'Didn't my maid tell you that I have guests?'

'Indeed, señora, she did.'

'Then what do you mean by insisting on interrupting me?'

'I am sorry, but I have to speak on an important matter. I understand that you knew Señor Cosgrove?'

'If I do, that is entirely my own business.'

'I am sure you will be very sad to learn that he went to sea in his motor-boat last night and that early this morning this boat was found abandoned. It seems almost certain he must have gone overboard.' He was astonished to see her sudden smile. 'Señora, perhaps you do not understand?'

'Kindly do not be impertinent.'

'But he has drowned.'

'If he fell into the sea, that surely is to be expected?'

'You did not like him?'

'I am not in the habit of either liking or disliking men of his character and background.'

'When he sailed out of the port he had a lady aboard.'

'Were the standard of your English higher, you would know better than to use the term "lady" to describe his female acquaintances.'

'Since she was not aboard when the boat was found, the question is where is she now and why has she not reported what happened? I think that perhaps he did not accidentally fall, but she pushed him overboard. If so, she must have disliked him very much.'

'There has never been the slightest difficulty in that.'

'You were in partnership with him, señora?'

Her mouth tightened one notch further.

'And you believed he had swindled you and you threatened to get your own back on him?'

'Are you suggesting ... ' Her voice rose and its tone became majestically incredulous. 'Are you daring to suggest that I would have set foot aboard his boat?'

'I am now asking you that, yes, señora.'

'My good man, do you not understand who I am?'

'Señora, I understand only that I have to learn certain things. So will you please explain where you were last night, between the hours of ten and midnight?'

'I certainly will not.'

'I must insist on you telling me.'

'Insist? You dare to use such a word to me?'

'Yes, señora.'

She was perplexed.

'Señora, surely it is easier to answer me now than to force me to arrest you?'

'To what?'

'You are a material witness and therefore must answer my questions. If you will not do so now, I have to take you before a judge and he will perhaps send you to jail if you still refuse to answer.'

'Jail?' she screeched.

'Let me try once more. Where were you last night?' Her eyes glistened with tears of mortification. 'I was with friends,' she finally muttered.

'When did you arrive there?'

'At eight.'

'And when did you leave?'

'Immediately after midnight.'

'What are the names of your friends?'

'You ... you can't go and ask them about me.'

He waited.

'Lord and Lady Menroth.'

'Where do they live?'

She gave their address.

'Thank you, señora, for your help,' he said, as he finished writing on the back of an old and crumpled envelope. As he said goodbye she gave him a look which made it clear that if given the chance she would not hesitate to push him over the side of a boat. And the further from shore, the better.

Chapter Twenty-Three

After watching a television film and drinking a last brandy, Alvarez said goodnight to the others and made his way up the stairs and through to the back bedroom. The shutters were not closed, and he sat down on the bed, switched off the light, and stared through the open window at Puig Antonia, softly outlined in the moonlight so that the sugar-loaf hill, with the hermitage on its crest, had an ethereal quality about it.

If only he could stop thinking about the case. A man had to be a real fool to go on and on worrying over an impossibility. Yet nothing would stop his brain questioning, wondering, checking ...

Had Cosgrove, after all, not been murdered? Had he pulled a twist upon a twist? Leading the police to believe he must be murdered so that he could laugh his way through to freedom? But Brenda had seen a woman aboard his boat, and it was surely impossible that he would have taken a woman with him when he fled, since she would then always have the power to betray him ... Yet if she hadn't gone with him either she also had had an accident or she had murdered him ...

Who was the woman? What motive could she have for murder? Since all those who had a motive for killing him because of the fraud believed him, on the authority of the police, to be dead, she could not be from his past in England. Yet to suppose the motive was unconnected with the fraud was to accept the 'coincidence' of a murderer giving entirely fresh cause for his own murder. Still, coincidences happened. Marta, Cosgrove's maid, had known a great deal about his private life, and she had said that any woman who had known him had had cause to hate him. But to hate was one thing, to murder another. (And in any case, Marta was demonstrably wrong; Gina Yearling had loved him.) True, the formidable Señora Newbolt would have had more than enough resolution to push him overboard, but who could ever mistake her figure, even in deceptive moonlight, and in any case she could not possibly have sailed on the boat. Marta had been unable to name any other woman with particular cause to hate him ...

So, to complete the circle, had he not been murdered: had fate and justice for once joined hands? ... But no woman was reported missing. Why had the woman aboard not reported the accident? Where was the boat's tender? ... Cosgrove must have been murdered.

He had once said to Brenda that when one met the impossible one should not turn back, one should press forward. But to press forward here was to put one's mind on the rack ...

He switched on the light, closed the shutters, undressed, put on his pyjama trousers, and lay on the sheet, too hot to need any bed-clothes over him. He switched off the light. No more thinking. Just drift off to sleep, to dream of the happiness which now, incredibly, was within his grasp ...

Perversely, his mind returned to the problem of solving the impossible. And then, for no immediately discernible reason, he began to suffer an indefinable fear, as if he were once more a small boy, terrified of a monster which might have used the darkness to creep close.

Through his fear there abruptly came the knowledge that he had been overlooking something that was surely vital ... Certain similarities about the murders of Moorhouse and Señorita Spiller had quickly linked them together on the grounds that a criminal so often repeated the method of his crimes when this had proved successful. Accept that Cosgrove had been murdered aboard the boat, and it was then obvious that an attempt had been made to present the murder as an accident: apparently the same pattern as before, suggesting the same murderer had struck for a third time. Yet the pattern had not been precisely the same. Aboard the boat there had been no skilfully planted clues designed to lead the police along a new and false trail which would inculpate an innocent person, should they have the wits to discover that there had been a murder, not an accident. So here, surely, was evidence that although the method used in the third murder seemed to link it to the first two as if one murderer had murdered thrice, in fact there had been two murderers. And this second murderer was someone who not only had had a sufficiently strong motive for murder but had also known sufficient of the details of the previous two murders to try and repeat them ...

Now the monster came out of the darkness to embrace him and to suffocate him with its foetid breath.

Brenda had told him her husband had guaranteed the debts of a friend who had over-invested in a firm which had sold property on the Peninsula. That firm had gone bankrupt, her husband had lost all his money and had committed suicide in a tragically mistaken gesture of sacrifice. She had as great, even greater cause to hate the two partners of the firm as had any of the hundreds who had bought their dreams in the sun, only to be swindled out of them ...

He had fallen in love with her and so had not hesitated to discuss the two murders: in particular, he could remember explaining in detail how the evidence had been set to make Miriam Spiller's death appear to have been an accident ...

The night he had had drinks with her in her flat, before going on to El Mar, he had mentioned the name of Beach and Thrush. At the time he had vaguely noted – a man in love was never sharp – that she had been surprised: he could now look back in time and be quite certain she had not been surprised, she had been shocked ... And later that night as, hand in hand, they had paddled through the sea, it had not been love which had made her wild, it had been memories ...

He groaned aloud. But the monster which gripped him was called Truth, and it was merciless.

*

When Alvarez came downstairs at eight the next morning, Dolores was cleaning the stove. Without looking round, she said: 'D'you want coffee – or there's some soup I can warm up, if you'd prefer it?'

'Nothing, thanks.'

'Why can't you men ever learn ... ' She turned and for the first time saw his face. She drew in her breath sharply. 'Mother of God, what is the matter? Are you in pain?'

'No.'

'But you're not feeling well? I'm going to call the doctor.'

'There's no need,' he said, with sudden harshness.

'You're so stubborn ... At least don't go straight off to work, but stay at home until you feel better.'

'I'm off now. To climb the Puig.'

'The Puig?' she repeated, her voice high. 'What is it? Is it her? Is she ill?'

'No.'

'Then has something happened between you?'

He hunched his shoulders.

She came forward and gripped his arm. 'Enrique, can I do something? I will do anything. We are not a great family, but we love and care for one another and surely that is worth much gold? I will explain this to her ... '

'It's not that sort of trouble.'

'Then what?'

'I cannot tell you.'

She dropped her arms. Her expression was now nearly as drawn as his.

*

He drove up the zigzagging narrow road which took him halfway up Puig Antonia, and then left the car in the very small parking area, partially blasted out of the rock. From here a mule track wound upwards past stunted bushes, patches of tall, brown, feathery weed grasses, and pine trees: a track worn smooth by countless mules and pilgrims. The view was magnificent but he did not see it, and as he climbed the sweat poured down his face, neck, and chest, and there was pain in his straining lungs and the calves of his legs: but it was right that he should suffer before he came into the presence of the saint.

On the relatively level top of the Puig were the many buildings of the hermitage, now deserted by hermits and looked after by nuns. Time had dealt severely with the buildings, and most were in need of repair.

Near the western edge was a small church, simple except for the altar, which was very ornate. He pushed open the heavy wooden door, crudely repaired with a plank, and entered, his breath whistling through his half-open mouth. To the right of the altar, under a bell-shaped glass set on a small marble plinth, was the worm-eaten, iron-bound wooden casket in which were the mortal remains of Santa Antonia. He knelt. Santa Antonia, he prayed, I am a man who has sinned much but always tried to make amends for his sins, who has known sorrow but tried to bear it bravely, who has recently found much happiness but tried to treat it lightly ... Answer me, now, when a man has to deny either himself or his duty, which does he deny?

He climbed the stairs to Brenda's flat very slowly, like an old man whose lungs and legs were nearly finished. He stood in front of the door of the flat for several seconds before he finally knocked, and even then it was more of a tap than a knock.

She opened the door and when she saw his face she drew in her breath sharply.

He stepped inside. 'Why did you tell me?' he demanded hoarsely.

She gave no answer.

'If you hadn't told me you'd seen the boat leave with a woman aboard I'd never have tried to find that woman, and found out the truth.'

Still silent, she led the way into the sitting-room. There, she went over to the sideboard and poured a brandy for him and a vermouth and soda for herself. She handed him the brandy, sat in the nearer armchair. She spoke for the first time in a small, strained voice: 'I want to say "Happiness", but ... Oh God, Enrique, why can the world be so bloody cruel?'

He slumped down in the second armchair.

'Please, you've got to try and understand,' she said.

'I understand only one thing: I love you. What else matters?'

'Enrique, you've got to see how it was. When I fell in love with Gerry it was both happiness and pain, only until he died I didn't realize that the pain was there. And after the pain there was hatred ... I hated the men who had made Gerry commit suicide so much that I used to pray they'd develop cancer ...

When I met you it was like starting life again after a long hibernation. I was scared and a little ashamed of my feelings at first, but then a veil seemed to come down over the past ... '

'When you told me you thought Blane, whom I hardly knew, was Anthony Moorhouse, a partner in Beach and Thrush, it was a hell of a shock, of course, and yet ... '

'And yet what?'

'And yet I did all I could to hide from you what a shock it had been.' Her voice had become low. 'Why did I do that?' she ended beseechingly.

He was too frightened by the implications of the probable answer to say anything.

She stared at him for a while, then shivered. When she next spoke, her voice was once more calm, and there might never have been that sudden outburst. 'But it didn't knock me for six as it would have done before I'd met you. Now there was this veil ... Nothing changed when you told me that Blane was Bonder, not Moorhouse.

And then I went into Palma and the plane was late, the luggage was further delayed, the passengers were moaning their heads off, and when we reached one of the hotels a brute of a man went on and on because he'd asked for a room overlooking the bay and he'd been given one facing the mountains ... By the time I'd coped with everyone I was utterly tired and sick of other people and their troubles, and so keyed up that I had to have a walk to try and calm down. If ... if only the plane hadn't been late, or the people so fractious, or I'd been less tired, I'd never have gone for that walk,' she said, with painful yearning.

If, he thought despairingly.

'I went up the harbour arm to look at the boats in the moonlight because they're always so beautiful in it, and someone hailed me from one of them. I must have been even more worn out than I thought because I didn't immediately recognize Blane. He asked me why I was walking the harbour in the middle of the night and then said that if I wasn't in a hurry to get to bed, why not go for a quick run with him? He was leaving in a day or two on a longish trip and had been working on the boat since the morning and now wanted to make certain everything was shipshape.

'I can't really explain now why I went aboard. The nearest I can get is that I wasn't thinking all that clearly and somehow I must have reckoned that by going and talking to him for a time – which I hadn't done before – I might begin to understand how any man could be so utterly vicious ...

We went out into the bay and then beyond the heads and it was all so beautiful in the moonlight and such a contrast to what had happened in the past that nothing seemed quite real. He was very amusing, in a smart-alecky way, about a lot of local people. I laughed quite a lot ... Then, when we were having a drink, he began to swing the conversation round, and suddenly I realized why he'd asked me aboard ... I was quite friendly with the detective who was investigating Miriam's death, wasn't I? Had he said how things were going? When I told him, no, you hadn't mentioned anything, he said, in that sardonic way of his, that when someone like Miriam was killed, her death was nearer to farce than tragedy.

I remembered how excited Miriam had been over becoming engaged, how she'd discovered for the first time in her life that the world could be wonderful, and that made me lose my temper. I told him he wouldn't have much longer to jeer at people because you *had* talked about the case to me and you were asking England if he were Colin Bonder.

He wasn't surprised, of course. He just said he'd no need to scramble, because like all Spaniards you were far too lazy to have actually got round to getting in touch with England. He was still playing at being the cynical, superior man who never flapped. I really believe he expected me to be impressed rather than shocked.

I told him who I was. That it had been Gerry's friend who had put up the money which had been lost in the swindle and that Gerry had guaranteed his friend's debts so that when the call had come, he had had to sell up everything, which had driven him to suicide. Blane stayed cynical and smart: said that it took an optimist to guarantee another person's debts, but a sentimental idiot to guarantee a friend's. The way he said it, his complete contempt for Gerry's standards, his indifference to Gerry's death ... Quite abruptly, that veil was gone and all the hurt and the hatred was back, even stronger than before.'

He said: 'Forget the rest and ... '

She interrupted him. 'He was standing on the wing of the flying bridge, just lighting a cigarette, when I walked over: d'you know, he was so self-satisfied that I think he believed I was coming to him because he was desirable! I pushed him in the chest and he went straight overboard, unbalanced by the rails.'

'He deserved to die,' he said violently.

Again, she seemed not to have heard him. 'He shouted once before he hit the sea. Then he shouted a lot more when he came back up to the surface. I could see his head, just clear of the boat's wake, in the moonlight and it reminded me of Joachim's head in *Salome* ... I put the engines to full ahead ... '

Her tone now expressed a measure of surprise. 'I didn't feel sick, or scared, or anything except quite satisfied that I'd done something unpleasant which had had to be done. And it was only quite a bit later that I began to wonder what I was going to do next.

I could be certain no one had seen me go aboard. I remembered what you'd told me about the murders and how he'd faked them to make them look like accidents and I decided I could do the same. I threw the glass I'd used overboard, together with the cigarette butts and the bottle of vermouth, and then poured a lot of the whisky over as well before leaving the bottle and his glass on the table. I dropped some grease on to the deck, pulled out one of the stanchions and left it hanging ...

I told you that Gerry had always loved boats and boating. I usually crewed for him so I knew quite a bit – at least enough not to be afraid of taking the tender, sailing into the bay, and landing in the middle, opposite the marshes, where there wasn't a soul for two or three kilometres. Then I stripped and took the tender back out and sank it in deepish water, swam ashore, waited until I was reasonably dry and walked back here.'

'So no one knows what happened.' He spoke urgently. 'I'll report that the eye-witness must have made a mistake and there almost certainly wasn't anyone else aboard when he sailed. I'll show how the false passport and boat's papers prove he pulled one last bluff, under the guise of an accidental drowning, in order to escape from the island and remain free.

That way, what will happen will be that Interpol will be alerted, but when he isn't found the case will gradually become forgotten history. No one but we two will ever know he isn't alive.'

'You're forgetting something. You're a policeman.'

He spoke violently. 'I am a man first of all. D'you imagine I could give anyone the evidence which would mean your arrest? ... I love you. I love you so that every day has become a magic day, as it was when we went wading in the sea ... Marry me. I know I can't offer much. I've no house, no land ... '

'If you'd a mansion and half the island I couldn't marry you.' Her voice was high, her expression strained.

'Why not?'

'Because I killed him.'

'If I'd been you, I would have killed him.'

'But you're not me, you're you, a detective. Can't you see — his death must always lie between us.'

'It means nothing ... '

'Enrique, please don't make it more difficult. I just can't marry you.'

He said, repeating the question he had put to her at the beginning: 'Why did you tell me there had been a woman aboard when the boat sailed?'

She finally answered him, in little more than a whisper: 'I suppose ... I suppose my conscience had begun to make a coward of me and I couldn't bear to live with the facts on my own: by telling you, I shifted some of the responsibility.'

Was that the truth? Or was the truth that when Cosgrove's words had stripped the veil from the past, they had also stripped it from the present? Had she discovered, even if only subconsciously, that she must find a way of bringing to an end a romance which for her could suddenly not be ... ?

Desperately, he tried to convince her she was wrong and that they could find happiness together, but in his heart he knew that he must fail.

Chapter Twenty-Four

The Calms of January delayed their arrival until February: the kind of chuckling perversity in which the island excelled. Days of blue skies succeeded one another, and only the slightest of breezes ruffled the clouds of late almond-blossom which from the air made the fields look as if snow had fallen.

Alvarez came downstairs and looked into the kitchen. 'I'm on my way ... '

'You'll sit down and have something hot to drink before you leave the house,' said Dolores firmly. 'Milk or coffee?'

He shrugged his shoulders.

'Enrique, you must ... ' She cut short the words when she saw the expression in his eyes. Her voice became soft. 'Sit down and I'll get you a decent breakfast.' She watched him slump down on to one of the kitchen chairs. He'd refused to tell anyone what had happened between Brenda and himself, but she could guess easily enough. Brenda had refused to marry a man who could offer her only his heart: in the final event she had turned out to be like all the other foreigners, wanting a large house, a shining new car ... 'There's a letter for you.' She went over to the refrigerator and picked it up from the top. Holding it rather as if it might contaminate her, she carried it across to him. 'It's from England.'

He took the envelope and stared at the neat, economical handwriting, then carefully slit it open with a knife and brought out the letter inside.

Brenda was very well, but had not yet got used to the weather. She couldn't seem to get warm unless she all but sat on the fire ...

Had he heard about the land? Before his death, Blane Cosgrove and Agnes Newbolt had formed a partnership to buy some land for which they'd hoped to be granted development permission. She couldn't understand exactly what had happened, but it seemed that the local council had been set against any development whatsoever, until an old man had died who had owned about half the foreshore of Cala Hispa, and his heir had turned out to be the mayor of Santa Veronica. Quite suddenly it had become clear that it must be in the interests of everyone to develop the land

166

and so provide much-needed jobs, and in consequence development permission for the whole cove had been granted. The land owned by the partnership had been sold to a Danish company for a tremendous profit, and as a result of this a large sum of money had come into Blane Cosgrove's estate. Because he had been guilty of fraud, this money had been sequestered (if that was the right word) by the English courts in order to repay as far as possible those he had defrauded. Quite a bit of the money Gerry had had to pay the bank had come through to her ...

You won't have to guess very hard to know the first thing I did! I bought a small farmhouse with fifteen acres. The house is almost in the middle of the land, without another place in sight, unless you look to the east. I've bought two cows – whose markings are rather odd and make me suspect their Jersey mothers were a bit flighty – which are giving almost five gallons of milk a day and it's so creamy that my figure is suffering badly.

The soil is medium loam, which tends to get a bit tacky in heavy rain, but otherwise works very easily. I've planned the garden – at the moment there's a pocket-handkerchief lawn and one overgrown rose-bed – and can't wait for spring when I'll get cracking ...

When you come to England you must visit the 'estate'. I know how much you'd love to walk over the grass and feel it springing beneath your feet, to feel the crumbly soil – if it's dryish! – and to admire the vegetables (obligatory to admire them) and to feed dairy cubes to my two house cows ...

He read to the end. He carefully folded the letter and replaced it in the envelope. He would never visit her, yet in his mind he would walk those green fields day after day.

*

Agnes, blue-rinsed midnight-black hair set in a very twirly fashion which might just have suited a winsome eighteen-year-old, sat with a friend at a table outside one of the front cafés in the port. She stared with brooding regret at the now empty glass dish in front of herself.

'Someone was saying yesterday that you've recently had some very good luck over land,' said her friend, with the sharp inquisitiveness of the born gossip.

'Luck?' Agnes looked up, her expression now one of annoyance. 'It wasn't anything to do with luck, it was sound judgement. And appreciating from the start what sort of a man Blane Cosgrove was so that he had no chance of swindling me.'

'Is it right that the land is at Cala Hispa and you've sold it for a big development?'

'Yes.'

'Tony says it's a very dramatic and lovely cove.'

'Quite possibly.'

'You've never been there?'

She ignored the question.

'Don't you feel that it's a bit of a shame to lose all that beauty by developing the place?'

Agnes said sharply: 'My dear Dorothy, there are some of us who aren't rich enough to be able to afford the luxury of being liberals.' A waiter came out of the café and she made up her mind suddenly and imperiously beckoned him across. 'I want another piece of chocolate layer cake, and make certain there's a decent amount of cream on it: last time, there was hardly any.' The waiter picked up the empty glass dish and returned inside.

Dorothy resumed talking, but Agnes didn't bother to listen. She stared out at the bay, heart-liftingly beautiful in the sharp sunshine, and she reflected with deep satisfaction that, as some obscure writer had once said, 'The gods are just.'

Printed in Great Britain
by Amazon